The
MAD KYOTO
SHOE SWAPPER
AND OTHER
Short Stories
from Japan

REBECCA OTOWA
with illustrations by the author

TUTTLE Publishing
Tokyo | Rutland, Vermont | Singapore

ABOUT TUTTLE
"Books to Span the East and West"

Our core mission at Tuttle Publishing is to create books which bring people together one page at a time. Tuttle was founded in 1832 in the small New England town of Rutland, Vermont (USA). Our fundamental values remain as strong today as they were then—to publish best-in-class books informing the English-speaking world about the countries and peoples of Asia. The world has become a smaller place today and Asia's economic, cultural and political influence has expanded, yet the need for meaningful dialogue and information about this diverse region has never been greater. Since 1948, Tuttle has been a leader in publishing books on the cultures, arts, cuisines, languages and literatures of Asia. Our authors and photographers have won numerous awards and Tuttle has published thousands of books on subjects ranging from martial arts to paper crafts. We welcome you to explore the wealth of information available on Asia at www.tuttlepublishing.com.

Published by Tuttle Publishing, an imprint of Periplus Editions (HK) Ltd.

www.tuttlepublishing.com

Copyright © 2020 Rebecca Otowa

Library of Congress Control Number:

ISBN 978-4-8053-1551-4

First edition
24 23 22 21 20
10 9 8 7 6 5 4 3 2 1   1911VP

Printed in Malaysia

TUTTLE PUBLISHING® is a registered trademark of Tuttle Publishing, a division of Periplus Editions (HK) Ltd.

Distributed by:

**North America,
Latin America & Europe**
Tuttle Publishing
364 Innovation Drive
North Clarendon
VT 05759 9436, USA
Tel: 1(802) 773 8930
Fax: 1(802) 773 6993
info@tuttlepublishing.com
www.tuttlepublishing.com

Asia Pacific
Berkeley Books Pte Ltd
3 Kallang Sector #04-01/02
Singapore 349278
Tel: (65) 6741-2178
Fax: (65) 6741-2179
inquiries@periplus.com.sg
www.periplus.com

Japan
Tuttle Publishing
Yaekari Building 3rd Floor
5-4-12 Osaki Shinagawa-ku
Tokyo 141 0032 Japan
Tel: 81 (3) 5437 0171
Fax: 81 (3) 5437 0755
sales@tuttle.co.jp; www.tuttle.co.jp

Contents

The Rescuer

I can tell what you're thinking. I know it's unheard of, committing something like this to writing. But I have received dispensation to record exactly what happened, before I begin my journey, because mine is a special case. Whoever ends up reading my report, I want to say that I believed I was acting for the best. First, I want to remember it all so it's clear in my mind. For the record, my name is Satoru Takeguchi, and I am an insurance agent working in central Tokyo.

I know where the story ends, but where it begins . . . that's a little more difficult. I guess I should start at the moment when I woke up on the train platform. At first I didn't know where I was. The light was so much brighter than I'd been used to, you see. It cascaded down in coruscations of gold. All the colors were much more glorious as well. For example, the yellow number 8 and the yellow triangle. They were closest to my eyes, and they glowed on the cement like the dust of a million suns. Another yellow thing caught my eye—a long strip with bumps on it. Following this, I saw that the brilliant golden numbers marched off into the distance, and beyond the bumpy strip I saw a sharp edge like a cliff face, where the cement just stopped. Beyond the edge, there was a misty blue space, like the gulf between distant mountains. It seemed so far down to the shining silver rails, laid across sharp reddish gravel. My eyes hurt from the magnificence of it.

Lying on the cement, right next to the yellow number 8, I saw a smartphone.

I recognized that smartphone. It was dull, scuffed silver, the screen blank and black. Peeping around the edge was a plastic zebra-striped case. Every detail of the phone was familiar to me. It was mine.

I figured I must have fainted and dropped the phone. Probably I got a bump on the head, and that was the cause of the change in my eyesight. I hurried to pick up my phone before anyone could step on it. I saw my arm reaching out, but somehow my hand couldn't pick the thing up. I tried several times, thinking I had bumped my hand as well as my head and numbed it, like when you hit your funny bone. This feeling was different, though. Not a flinching flash of painful sensation in my elbow or a tingling in the wrist. Just . . . nothing. I was puzzled. How could I have hurt myself so badly I didn't even feel any pain? I thought I'd go and find some help.

I stood up slowly, with my feet on either side of the smartphone to keep it from being stepped on. That was when I noticed that there was no one nearby. Turning carefully, I saw that a small crowd had congregated at the front of a train which was stopped on the other side of the platform behind me. The light and the colors were still blinding, but the sound of the scene came up only gradually. I began to hear exclamations, and one or two women were screaming breathlessly. Suddenly a brilliant flash of light rushed past me—two men dressed in white, with a stretcher between them piled with blankets. A group of policemen followed closely behind. Like the light and the colors, the movement of the men was so intense it made me dizzy. The policemen hustled the crowd aside while the men in white jumped down in front of the train and busied themselves with something there.

Gradually, I noticed more details. An ashen-faced man in a dark uniform with a peaked cap was being helped to one of the platform seats by a kind old lady. The crowd was pushed farther back by train officials who were stringing yellow tape across the front of the train. Other officials hurried down the aisle inside the train and motioned the passengers to get off. Some of them tried to go forward and take a look, but they were firmly prevented. They moved slowly down the platform toward the stairs, many of them dazed, others avid, talking excitedly, craning backward for a glimpse. Then, one after the other, almost all of them started to use their smartphones. That characteristic pose with neck bent, one hand holding the phone, thumb working away at the buttons. Probably texting their friends about the unexpected blip in their day.

After a few minutes, the white-uniformed men maneuvered the stretcher, now heavy and full, onto the platform. Their uniforms were daubed with red dust, and the knees were soaked in red as well. In the blazing light that fell on everything, it was clear to me that those spots were someone's blood—the blood of the person who now lay on the stretcher covered with blankets. This blood seemed to glow with a baleful energy. As the men passed me with their burden, something slipped out of the blankets and dangled off the stretcher. No one noticed but me.

Yes, I noticed all right. I recognized the shirt sleeve. My favorite blue and white striped shirt, now torn and grimy. I knew it was mine because the cuff button was undone, and hanging by a thread. The shirt, and the dead arm that was wearing it, belonged to me.

I was dead.

Everything began to make sense.

I looked down at the phone lying at my feet, trying to feel a connection between it and the hand I had just seen dangling out of a blue and white cuff. Suddenly, a reaching arm appeared, and the phone was whisked away. Right next to me—I could almost feel their breath—a policeman held it out toward a white,

shaking girl. "Is this the one?" he asked her.

"Yes," she quavered. "He was walking along, looking at his phone, the way everyone does, when he lost his footing just as the train came in. Ohhh . . . " She closed her eyes and swallowed. "When he fell, the phone went flying in the air."

The policeman nodded. He glanced toward the scene of the accident, figuring out the distance, then picked up the phone. "Please take a seat," he called over his shoulder to the girl. "We will need to get a statement." She sank into a seat next to the white-faced man, who was now bent forward, his shoulders shaking. I realized he must be the train driver.

I watched the rest of the scene play out. Another driver appeared and the train rumbled off. The police escorted the girl and the train driver away down the platform. I heard a few PA announcements saying the station was temporarily closed and service suspended because of an accident. Pretty soon the place was deserted.

I thought I'd better leave too. I wanted to follow my body and see where it was being taken. I could move, it felt just like ordinary walking, though it had been obvious in the last few minutes that no one was aware of me. However, I soon discovered that I couldn't leave the station. Every time I tried to climb the stairs, I found myself back on the platform again. It was like an endless loop. I wondered what to do next. I went down to the place where the accident had occurred. Nothing was to be seen but a large patch of fresh blood on the red gravel and the silver train track. It was horribly disturbing, and somehow alluring.

That was my blood. No use to me anymore, yet it was part of me, and I didn't want to leave it there. It seemed kind of lonely.

Eventually, two men in work clothes appeared, dragging a long blue hose between them. They hopped down onto the tracks, turned on the hose, and began washing the blood away. I sat on a nearby seat and watched them. When they were finished, they left.

I sat on. The light was tyrannously bright outside, but under the roof of the platform was an island of cool blue shade. It was very peaceful. Early morning became late morning. I began to remember the last moments of my life. I was on my way to work at the insurance company, where I had been hired as a new recruit the previous year. I sifted through the contents of my brain as it had been that morning—little snippets: my girlfriend's hair lit by street lamps as we walked home after dinner last night, the aftertaste of the rice ball I had gulped down for breakfast, the slight irritation on my chin caused by my new electric shaver. Since it was summer, I hadn't been wearing a suit coat. All of Tokyo was in its shirt sleeves. No tie, either. I liked summer because of the slightly more relaxed dress code; but I always wore long sleeves because the air conditioning at the office was a little too cold for me. That morning, in my solitary apartment, I had put on the blue and white striped shirt, and I noticed that the button of the cuff was about to come off. But I also knew that if I stopped to fix it then, I would be late for my train. So I decided to do it after work that night. I had left the button undone because I thought the buttonhole would tear it off and I would lose it altogether. Such a tenacious little white button. It had hung on grimly throughout the drama of my death.

I saw the last moment of my life. Walking along, head bent, holding the phone with my left hand while with the right I stroked the screen, looking for a text message from my girlfriend. My feet straying across the yellow bumps of the Braille blocks, closer and closer to the edge. The left foot in its black business shoe missing the platform edge, pawing thin air. The sudden looming bulk of the train, and the roaring noise. It all happened so quickly. I didn't feel anything.

I sat there on the platform seat, reliving it. I wondered if it was okay to call it "reliving it" when you were dead. In one second, my life was gone. I didn't feel sad, or cheated, or resentful. It was just an occurrence, like not buttoning my button that morning, or cupping my girlfriend's face in the bluish light of the street lamp, just before her warm kiss. Dying was another experience of my life.

But now, for some reason, I was stuck at the scene of my death. My poor broken body could leave, but I couldn't.

Was there a reason I was still here? Something I needed to see, to notice? I gazed around and realized that the station had opened again. Passengers were beginning to wander around on the platform, avoiding the patches of summer sunlight and staying in the shade. Some were buying drinks from the vending machine, others lining up at the edge of the platform, fanning themselves or wiping their sweaty necks with handkerchiefs. I heard the swish of summer dresses and the crisp crackle of new-ironed shirts; I saw the pretty, delicate sandals of women and the boat-like, comically long shoes of men. And of course, lots of them were looking at their phones. The universal pose of modern man. If we don't watch out, our spines will curve back into a Neanderthal shape, and our evolution will start going backwards. I chuckled at the thought, and at that moment, a young guy in dreadlocks passed me. Of course he wouldn't have heard me even if I'd been alive. He was bopping to music only he could hear, his ears firmly plugged by earphones as he flicked his phone screen with his fingers.

There was a PA announcement for the next train. The music that signaled the approach of a train began tinkling, the railroad crossing began pinging. It seemed very noisy to me, but most people didn't seem to notice the noise. They walked along oblivious, glued to their phones. I wasn't oblivious, though. My phone-staring days were over. I watched the people.

Oh my god.

A young girl, beautiful clean hair swinging around her bent face, was strolling along the extreme edge of the platform grinning at something on her phone's screen. She wasn't looking. She was going to go over. Her feet, in high-heeled platform sandals, got closer and closer to the edge—the train was coming in . . .

Before I knew what I was doing, I took a huge breath, filling my lungs, and shouted in a great, booming voice. "Look out!"

Somehow, it worked. The young girl looked up, realized she was in danger, and swerved away from the edge just as the train roared in. She didn't seem that concerned; she was looking at her phone again almost immediately. Other people nearby hadn't seemed to hear me. Of course I hadn't physically shouted. It was like a blast of energy I was somehow able to aim directly at her.

That's when I knew why I'd been unable to leave the platform. I had work to do here. I had to rescue people who were in danger of falling off the edge because they were staring at their phones. I wasn't sure how long I would have to do it, but this was my destiny. I sagged with relief and depleted energy—one person had been saved—but then I became vigilant again. It was my duty to make sure that at this station, right now, another one of these people wouldn't become a pool of fresh blood and a blanket-covered mound, because of a second of carelessness.

Time passed. After I had been at the station for a day and a night, I began to be comfortable with my situation. I strolled up and down the platform, taking my ease between trains, observing this person and that. I enjoyed the colors of the air around them and the music of their voices. But when a train was due I was all attention, raking my gaze across the crowd, looking for inattentive phone users. Most of them confined their wanderings to the center of the platform where they were in no danger; but still, that first day, I saved two other people—a middle-aged man trying to connect to WiFi and a university student who had just discovered a site featuring naked women. (I was starting to be able to see what they were looking at on their phones, as well.) I was getting quite skillful at aiming the warning blast of energy, and both times the men looked up and around in time to save themselves from tumbling into the path of the approaching train. I felt almost like a station employee, one no one could see. I wondered why the big stations didn't hire people to do this very job, to stem the increasing tide of phone-related accidents. I didn't see any living person attempt to save or caution anyone else. Of course, they were mostly looking at their own phones. How oblivious they all were, as if they were each traveling in their own impenetrable bubble of space. I didn't see them this way; to me, they were all connected by tiny details—resemblances of hand or ear, bag or hat, print of shirt or blouse. They were like drops in an ocean of humanity. But they didn't understand this—they all thought they were alone and all-important.

The following day, I pulled off a more complicated rescue. Just as the next train was due, I spotted a young man walking along very slowly, completely engrossed in his screen. His phone screen was alive with jumping and cavorting game figures and he was determined to win. Nothing else mattered. He was walking along the bumpy yellow blind man's strip—and just then, up behind him came an actual blind man. He was walking the strip with confidence—I guess he did this every day—his cane just lightly tapping in front of him. Quite rapidly he walked, and soon closed the distance with the slowpoke gamer. Just as he was about to ram into him from behind, I achieved an amazing feat. I actually aimed a blast of energy at both of them at once! The blind man stopped short, and by the time he'd recovered and started walking again, the gamer had shifted off the yellow strip. He was still playing his game, but he was now out of the other man's way. Accident averted. I felt quite proud of myself.

You might be wondering what I did at night, when there

were no trains or passengers or phone users. Well, of course I didn't need to sleep. I used to sit on the platform seat and just feel the energy all around me. It was quite beautiful. This particular station happened to be in the middle of a relatively residential area, considering it was central Tokyo, and what I found most amazing were the dreams of the sleepers in the beds in the apartment buildings that surrounded the station. It was like watching hundreds of movies at once, or maybe like a fireworks display or a kaleidoscope. I couldn't zoom in on any one person, but still, it was fascinating. All those dreams, all that life, streamed upward from the buildings, out the windows and doors, and seeped through the roofs like many-colored auroras. It was really lovely. I used to sit there entranced for hours at a time.

All right. Now I have to tell what happened on the third day. This is really the end of my story, though it isn't the end of the story, if you know what I mean. You don't? You soon will. Keep reading.

It was midmorning, and the train platform wasn't very crowded. At that time of day it was mostly middle-aged or elderly people, off to the museum or lunch with their friends. And because it was the older generation, there weren't too many smartphones among them. A few had those clamshell phones, but they aren't nearly as mesmerizing as smartphones because they don't have as many functions, and also their displays aren't as bright or interesting. Since my death, I'd been mulling over the possibility that the smartphone inventors actually program some sort of addictive component into the display. It certainly is uncannily hard to look away.

Along came a fiftyish woman, beautifully dressed, walking slowly along in The Pose, frowning at the display of her smartphone. I noticed it was a brand new one. She was even more rapt than an ordinary phone user, probably because she was still learning how to use it. In fact her concentration was tinged with annoyance. Something wasn't right with her phone—it wasn't doing what it was supposed to. I used to wonder why older people got so annoyed at their electronic devices, but now I saw the reason. Older people were used to having the tools they used obey them. They thought of them as servants. But these new devices could disobey their owners. In a way, they weren't the servants, but the masters. Everyone had to learn how their devices liked things to be done. People had to adapt to the rigorous paradigms of their machines. This was a fundamental shift in human experience, and older people hadn't yet succeeded in adapting their thought patterns to the lockstep rhythm of their devices. Their brains were still organic, and they expected the machines to act organically too.

In her trance, the woman was drifting closer and closer to the edge of the platform.

Since she was older, and so very fixated on her phone, I decided to warn her a little early—the train had been announced, but it wasn't in range of sight or hearing yet. I fired off a blast—but she kept right on going. No reaction. I fired off another one. The approach music began. Time was getting short. I fired off a third one, as strongly as I could. I had never had to do this before and was getting a bit anxious. The woman was done for if I couldn't get her attention. I heard the train approaching, but she didn't seem to notice. Her feet had crossed the blind man's strip and hovered on the edge. Her gaze never left the screen. And this gave me my great idea.

Summoning all the energy I had at my disposal, I concentrated on the woman's phone screen. I fired off a blast stronger than ever before, and succeeded in making my face appear on her screen. But—too late—I realized that what appeared was the face I had died with: bloody, smeared and broken. It was hideous, contorted in the snarl of death. I had wanted to use my face to warn her, but instead this awful thing filled her vision.

She reeled backward on her high heels, fortunately away from the platform's edge, and fell heavily to the ground. At first

I was elated—at least she hadn't fallen into the path of the train. But she wasn't moving. Her hand clutched the phone, once, twice, and then loosened and the phone fell to the pavement. Her eyes were closed and her face twisted with pain.

Another passenger, a few meters away, cried out in surprise and rushed forward. It was an efficient-looking man. He bent down, took the woman's pulse, and called out to another passenger to phone for an ambulance. "She's had a heart attack, I think!"

I watched in horror, rooted to the spot. People rushed past and through me as the wail of an ambulance got louder and louder. A couple of station officials appeared, pushing past the small ring of people that had gathered around the fallen woman. I heard the efficient man, who still knelt next to her, say, "Yes, she's dead."

What had I done? Instead of saving the woman, I had killed her. My awful bloody face had scared her to death. I didn't know what to do.

Then I felt a tap on my shoulder. I had not been touched since I had died, so it was a great surprise. I whirled around, and found myself looking into the face of the woman. She was lying on the ground a little way away, but she was also standing there, looking into my eyes.

"You can go now," she said to me. Then, with great calm, she walked over and sat down on one of the platform seats.

I found I was now able to leave the station. In fact, as soon as the words left her lips, I began to feel that I was floating upward. A period of amorphous sensation followed, and the next thing I knew, I was here, sitting at this desk. A Wise One appeared and explained to me that my job was over. It had been handed over to the next person to die at that station. That woman would now assume the task of warning inattentive smartphone users of their danger, until another death occurred and the next dead person took over.

"That's the way it works," he said. "Usually, some negligence is involved in the handover. The rescuer is distracted for a moment, or he is ultimately unable to get the phone user's attention. But in your case, you were actively involved in the woman's death. That's unusual, and it's the reason why we are giving you the opportunity to write an account of the incident."

"But aren't you going to blame me?" I stammered. "I failed to save her. In fact, I killed her. Don't I have to be punished?"

"No. Her heart attack was imminent anyway. She realized that, and she took full responsibility for her own death. She requested to take over from you because she knew that you believed you were acting for the best. You were, weren't you?"

"Of course," I answered, relieved. "I had no idea that horrible thing would happen. I was just trying to get her attention and save her."

"Yes, we understand. And so does she. There is no cause for punishment, and you have accrued no karma from your action. If anything, this incident has clarified for us the terrible power of the smartphone screen. We must redouble our efforts."

"So what happens now?"

"Well, as soon as you have finished writing your account, you will be free to begin your journey."

That's exactly what I'm going to do. Now that I've got it all clear in my mind, I'm going to write my report, and then I'll be off. Thank you for your attention.

Genbei's Curse

1948

A winter's washing day. Splinters of sunlight reflected upward from puddles between the courtyard flagstones onto the weathered eaves. Two wooden laundry buckets stood side by side, one of them steaming with soapsuds and a wooden washboard sticking out.

Sachiko plunged her red wrinkled hands into the other bucket, which was full of cold rinse water, and snagged an elusive hand towel. Wringing it out—a sharp tug of both wrists in opposite directions—produced a twinge in her shoulders that made her wince. She straightened slowly from her crouching

position and reached to pin up the towel. Long-familiar movements, repeated too often. Her whole body was a complex choir of small, thrumming pains. The evening bath sometimes helped, if the water hadn't gone tepid by the time it was her turn.

Gently pounding both hips with wet fists, Sachiko surveyed her work. All around her, dripping clothes hung like wrinkled ghosts. Belly bands, sleeveless undershirts, children's flannel trousers, dishtowels, bathing towels, and an endless procession of limp, grayish old men's undershorts. The chore was the same every day, but today she had won the weather lottery—the strong sunshine was beginning to tease little tendrils of vapor from the folds of the hanging clothes. The laundry would dry without having to be hung up over the stove in the kitchen later.

Sachiko grasped the edge of the wash bucket to tip the water across the flagstones, when a harsh voice rang out. "Don't tip that water out! You aren't finished!" Genbei, her father-in-law, had lurched his way out onto the open verandah, grasping a pillar with one chalky hand and holding a wad of dingy cloth in the other.

Oh god, he's wet himself again, was Sachiko's first thought. But no, it was worse than that. The brown stains and the dreadful odor told their own story. Sachiko drew back involuntarily.

"You come here! Useless girl!" the old voice cawed. "Don't I get an answer? Such bad manners!"

"Yes, Father. I'm sorry," Sachiko murmured without moving toward him.

"It's your cooking—so bad I got a stomachache and couldn't make it to the toilet in time. Now get these washed. And come and change my futon covers too. Hurry up! I'm cold." He flung the clothes down onto the flagstones and his unsteady old man's footsteps receded down the verandah.

Gritting her teeth, Sachiko transferred the clothes to the wash bucket with the extreme ends of her fingers. The water no longer steamed. She hurried into the kitchen and set the big kettle on the fire, then down the hall with an armload of fresh linen to the old man's bedroom.

The room was dim and stuffy, and stank of charcoal fumes and excrement. Holding her breath, Sachiko worked silently, changing the bed linen with abrupt, nervous movements. Genbei huddled over the *hibachi* charcoal brazier and glared malevolently at her. Insults erupted from him like boiling water spitting from an overfilled kettle. "Stupid. Ugly. What was my son thinking. He could have gotten ten better wives without even lifting his hand. Bad-mannered. Terrible cook. Worse housekeeper."

Finally Sachiko was finished. "There you are, Father, all nice and clean," she said as she hurried to the doorway, taking a huge lungful of fresh air from the passage. "You lie down and I'll make you a nice cup of tea." She could still hear him muttering as he lowered himself carefully onto the futon.

Her back renewed its complaints when she lifted the heavy kettle and carried it outside to replenish the wash bucket. The steaming water splashed onto the reeking linens, and she scrubbed them furiously without looking at them. A few tears fell into the murky water. Sachiko didn't even notice that she was crying again.

After washing her hands several times, Sachiko took the old man his tea and then slumped at the *kotatsu* heated table. The clock ticked and the hibachi beside her whispered occasionally as the charcoal shifted. Raising her hand to brush the hair from her forehead, she imagined she smelled a whiff of excrement. With a convulsive movement she got up and washed her hands once more, then rubbed them with a drop of camellia oil from her secret stash under the washbasin.

Her eyes went to the black-framed photograph of her mother-in-law on the wall. *Oh Mother*, she whispered, you *are well out of it. Why did you die and not me? You were the one to tend to Father's every need, to make the delicacies he loved, to arrange his teacups and futons and hibachi just so. You were the one who spoiled him, treating him like an invalid even though he isn't. And now you've deserted me. You've gone to the Pure Land and I'm left in hell.*

The sight of the smiling old lady did give some comfort, Sachiko had to admit. She had been a truly good soul. Now that she was gone, Sachiko tried to live up to her memory, but it was an uphill struggle. Worse, she was mostly alone with Genbei, because his yelling drove her husband and children away. Yujiro stayed longer and longer at his small business in town; the children stayed out playing at their friends' houses. Only Sachiko was left, stuck, trapped, a drudge at the beck and call of a senile old man.

Suddenly the silence skittered away like a frightened cat. "Sachiko! Girl! Sachiko!"

Sachiko stuck out her tongue in the direction of the voice and heaved herself upright. With leaden steps she trudged down the hall and put her head around the door of Genbei's room. "What is it?"

"Too much tea." Genbei threw back the quilt to reveal a huge wet patch on the fresh clean linen. His crotch was also sodden. The hot smell of urine rose in the turgid air. Stunned, Sachiko looked at the old man's face. His lips were stretched over his toothless gums and his old eyes were twinkling. Was he actually grinning? Sachiko's brittle discipline shattered like a pane of glass, and the demons of hysteria came hurtling out. She began to shriek.

"No! No!! NO!!!" Her hair whipped across her face as she shook her head violently. "You are *disgusting!* I'll never wash your underwear again! Not one more piece of clothing, not one more futon cover! *Never! Never!* I'll die before I do!" She whirled toward the door.

"Oh yes?" the old man shouted. He tottered to his feet, his eyes burning, and stretched out one bony arm. "Then I curse you! Get out! Get out! You are no longer a member of this family! You *will* die—you'll die in a ditch! *I curse you!*"

With a gasp of horror, Sachiko banged the door shut and pounded down the corridor as if a million devils were after her.

An hour later she was still sitting at the kotatsu, her head on her arms, listening to her pounding heart as it gradually resumed its normal rhythm. Finally she raised her head and realized that daylight was fading: the house was utterly silent. She really ought to see if the old man was all right, but she couldn't make herself go back there.

With a clatter the front door slid open and Yujiro's voice came faintly. "I'm home." He entered the room and stopped when he saw Sachiko's face. "What's the matter?"

"Father . . ." she whispered. Yujiro turned immediately and his heels pounded along the wooden corridor toward the bedroom. The footsteps returned, quickly, and Yujiro paused in the doorway. Sachiko wanted to turn and look at him, but her neck would not move.

"He's unconscious," he muttered, his voice thin with shock. "I'll go use Mrs. Yoshida's phone." He went out, sliding the door closed softly, like a person at a funeral. In a moment she heard his footsteps go by outside, on the path between their house and the neighbors'.

Sachiko got up and slowly prepared a simple evening meal. When it was ready, she put it on the table, covered it with a cloth, and went to her own room. She lay down and pulled the quilt over her head. The winter dark came down around her. She lay quaking with shame and terror, unable to get the curse out of her mind. Did such things really happen? Only in morality tales for children, surely? If only she hadn't started that stupid quarrel. Just a little more *gaman*, one last teaspoonful of endurance, would have gotten her through. And then maybe the old man wouldn't have collapsed.

The thumping and bumping that followed a little later, as Genbei was carried off to the ambulance, were muffled by the quilt, but Sachiko heard everything.

Genbei had had a stroke. He was now a true invalid. He lay all day in his room, unable to get up unassisted, wound in a clumsy cloth diaper. A local woman was hired to take care of the old man and to wash his mountains of laundry. Sachiko was horrified at herself, but somehow she remained adamant. She never touched another piece of his stinking linen again. She washed the family's clothes separately. She never went into Genbei's bedroom unless it was unavoidable, and she never spoke to him.

Sachiko told her husband the story of that awful morning, and for once he didn't say she was crazy or just making things up. But the local woman was expensive, and money grew tighter. The villagers gossiped. After all, plenty of people had aged parents to take care of. Why were they wasting money on a servant?

Old Genbei finally died after another stroke. He had not spoken another word since the day he cursed his daughter-in-law. Neighbors who came in to help get the house in shape for the funeral whispered to each other and looked askance at Sachiko, who seemed to have gone gray overnight. Meanwhile the story of the curse had somehow spread through the neighborhood. People discussed it in undertones, half horrified and half amused.

1998

Sachiko lay in bed. Her comfortable old futons had been placed on a wooden platform to make it easier to care for her. The bright, clean sunshine of another winter filtered through the *shoji* paper screen at her side, but the bedroom itself smelled of sickness and age. She had been in this bed for a year, a prisoner of a wasting disease. Alone, widowed, and old—with only her son and his wife, who had moved in when she became bedridden, to care for her.

A sudden sharp vision came to her, of her own struggles with the daily chores, so long ago. As far back as she could remember, she had been perpetually on the verge of tears. The difficulties of her life had loomed so large that they had crowded out all her other experiences. She now had trouble remembering a single happy moment with Yujiro, her children, or her garden.

Through her pain and weakness, Sachiko became aware of another sensation. She had to go to the bathroom. She needed help to get out of bed, but there was no sound nearby—her daughter-in-law must be in another part of the house, and there was no way to call her.

Helplessly, Sachiko felt the warm urine seep out of her into the futon. As the smell wafted up to her nostrils, she recalled the day of Genbei's curse. This, this moment right now, was the real curse—to be useless, unnecessary and helpless, just an old body in a wet bed, waiting to die.

The wet bedclothes gradually cooled and Sachiko began to shiver. It seemed like ages before her daughter-in-law, Shinobu, knocked timidly and came into the room. "Lunchtime soon, Grandmother," she said.

Sachiko suddenly found that she was in a towering rage. Her trembling body glowed with the heat of it. "About time you checked on me!" she cried in a cracked voice, struggling to sit up. "I need you to change the bed linen. You were off somewhere and I couldn't call you when I had to go. Where on earth have you been? Useless girl!"

Shinobu, who was slight and small-boned, seemed to shrink further under the scolding. She scurried without a word to the closet to get out clean bedding, and avoided her mother-in-law's eyes as she helped her into the bedside chair. Then she got to work, stripping off the old woman's soaked nightgown with abrupt, nervous movements, and sponging her off. After she'd put Sachiko into a fresh nightgown and changed the bed linen, she helped her back into bed. "I'll have lunch ready in a minute," she whispered as she scurried out with an armload of soiled linen.

Sachiko felt her rage gradually melt away. She looked at a bar of sunlight lying across the clean quilt cover. It suddenly blurred as tears filled her eyes. This was different from the chronic weeping she had done as a young woman. These were not tears of self-pity but of understanding. She wept for herself, for her daughter-in-law, for the old man who had been so miserable, for everyone who ever needed something they couldn't get. She sobbed as if her heart would break.

Maybe it did crack a little . . . a tiny seed of gratitude was pushing its way up within her heart. A strange, unusual sensation. Genbei's curse hadn't worked. Here she was, still alive. She hadn't died in a ditch. She felt her warm, dry clothes, the comfort of the soft bed, the glory of the winter sunshine. But just for a moment she had tasted her father-in-law's helpless rage on her own tongue. She had used the exact words that she herself had flinched under, all those years ago. The realization dried up her tears in a moment and she lay staring into space.

The door slid open again and Shinobu entered, balancing a tray. She put it down on the bedside table, avoiding Sachiko's eyes, clearly wanting to get out again as soon as possible. Sachiko was so sharply reminded of herself as a young woman that she felt her eyes fill with tears again. It was now or never. Break the curse. Break the silence. She forced herself to speak.

"Excuse me. I'm sorry I shouted at you. You do so much for me. I am grateful." Shinobu turned and looked at the old woman with surprise, and a little suspicion. Sachiko continued, "When you are finished eating lunch, can you come and talk to me for a minute? I'd like to discuss this business of my incontinence. Maybe we can find a solution that will be best for both of us." Shinobu nodded and left.

Sachiko snuggled down in the bedclothes, relishing the warmth, her old eyes resting now with pleasure on the sunlit quilt cover. No more crying. She would make a clean breast of the past. Only the truth would do, and she would tell it all to her daughter-in-law. It was time to lift Genbei's curse.

Trial by Fire

May 25, 1619

"That is unacceptable!"

Kisuke straightened his back, folded his arms, and glared at his opponent on the other side of the wooden meeting hall, where the two groups of disputants were lined up facing each other. Behind him, the men of the Eastern faction murmured discontentedly. Kisuke hated the lounging posture and slurred words of the Western leader, Kakubei. Didn't he have any respect for this gathering?

The mediator in the center cleared his throat. "Does anyone else have anything to say?" Kisuke could tell that the man was poised to jump to his feet and scurry out the door. Of course, he was neutral, neither Eastern nor Western, appointed by the regional government. But being neutral might not save him from a beating after the meeting broke up and frustrated men were walking home in the darkness. No wonder he was in a hurry to leave while it was still light.

"I call upon the representatives to sum up their positions. The subject under dispute is right of access to the forests of Mount Toyama and adjoining peaks. Western faction, will you be the first to sum up your position? Please be brief."

Kakubei, that rude and lounging man, stood up. "The Western faction appeals to the sense of fairness of our Eastern cousins. We on the flat lands have no mountains of our own. How are we to obtain the firewood, the charcoal, the plants and animals we need for our lives, if we are denied the right of access to the mountain?" He sounded plausible, but his aggressive stare robbed the words of their politeness.

At the mediator's signal, Kisuke rose to his feet. "We of the Eastern faction have tried many times to compromise with the West. We have suggested allowing access for a certain number of days each season so that they can gather what they need. But the Western faction demands unlimited rights. This is not reasonable. These mountains rise from the very doorsteps of the Eastern villages. They have been our property since the time of our illustrious ancestors. Will our friends in the West not respect the ancient ways? We repeat that we are willing to grant road access to the mountain range for an agreed-upon interval in each season. But it is not large enough to support unlimited access by both factions all year long. The plants and mushrooms and wood would be used up within a year, and then what will we all do? If this does not meet with agreement, I suggest that the men of the Western faction request access from other villages at the foot of the mountain range. There is no need to insist on our village."

The room erupted, red-faced men leaning toward each other and shouting. "The East is cruel!" "The West is greedy!" "We do not accept the terms!" Gradually, the angry voices subsided. Kisuke sat down at the center of a swirling river of emotion. He glanced out the door, where an early summer sunset was bathing the countryside in golden-green light. A couple of house martens swooped under the eaves. It was time for the meeting to adjourn and all the tired men to go home.

The mediator spoke. "This dispute will not be resolved tonight. I ask the factions to reconsider their positions and convene here again on the evening of the next full moon. This meeting is concluded." He gathered his papers into a roll and hurried to the exit.

Kisuke took his time. He locked eyes with Kakubei. The man wasn't even a native of the area. Who knew where he had come from? The Western faction rose in a body and left, murmuring. When the last one had shuffled into his straw sandals and stepped out into the sunset. Kisuke turned to his neighbor, the elderly Kurazaemon.

"This dispute is going on too long. What can we do? The whole region is in an uproar."

The old man regarded him solemnly. "We can do nothing right now. Neither side is prepared to concede an inch."

"If nothing can be done, we may have to appeal to the central government to arbitrate. Our regional officers have no neutrality. They are all involved on one side or the other, or else their relatives are."

"I know this. The government in Edo, though—what do they know of the problems we face in the provinces? Have they ever walked the forest glades? No. They have probably never even waded in the mud of a rice field. They know only the cobbles of city streets and the polished corridors of the courts." Kurazaemon prepared his old legs for standing, and laid a hand on Kisuke's shoulder for support. "Ah!" he grunted, pushing himself upright. "This new government causes more trouble than it's worth. No respect for the old ways."

New government? thought Kisuke, helping the old man to the door. It had been almost a whole generation since the Tokugawa clan unified the country under the shogunate in Edo. He himself could hardly remember a time when they weren't in power, though old men like Kurazaemon had survived the bloody and turbulent war years. "Well, it can't be helped. We must try to find a solution before the next meeting. Otherwise, who knows? The Western faction may send brigands through our villages to take what they want by force."

"That can't be allowed," agreed Kurazaemon, and they parted in the dooryard of the meeting hall. Kisuke stumped home through the fragrant twilight, his thoughts turning to his supper.

June 23, 1619

The next full moon fell on the longest day of the year. The men splashed cool water on their faces and hands at a row of buckets the women had set outside the door of the meeting hall. Kisuke noticed that the men of the Western faction took their places with a subtle air of excitement. What were they up to now?

"The discussion of this subject will now resume," the mediator announced. "I understand the Western faction has a new suggestion. We will hear from Kakubei first, and then everyone will discuss the proposal."

Kakubei got to his feet and struck a dramatic pose, raising both fists into the air. "Men of the East, you have spoken of the importance of the old ways. What I propose harks back to deepest antiquity. Since we cannot come to an agreement by words, I propose a traditional trial by fire." A storm of exclamations arose on every side. The mediator rapped on the wooden floor for quiet.

Kisuke rose as well. "What do you mean by that?"

"In the old days, this kind of dispute was settled by an ordeal undergone by two representatives, one from each side. You must have heard of this."

"Yes, but the last of these ordeals was decades ago, in a far-off province. I heard the story from a traveling merchant when I was just a young man. The government has put a stop to all such trials."

"Since the last meeting, I have been making inquiries," Kakubei retorted. The central government is prepared to make a special dispensation, since our case seems to be unsolvable by ordinary means."

Kisuke's brow darkened. What right had Kakubei to make these inquiries behind his back? And what right had the government to rescind their own law discontinuing these outmoded ordeals? The Edo government might be stern, but at least it had imposed rules on society which were, for the most part, reasonable. Kisuke was sure that no one really wanted to go back to the bad old days.

"Exactly what form of ordeal is being suggested?" he asked.

"The trial would consist of two contestants, each endeavoring to carry a red-hot iron ax in his bare hands, from a brazier to the altar of Watamuki Shrine. Whichever contestant succeeds, or goes the farthest, would be the winner and the faction he represents would carry the day." Kakubei paused, and added impressively, "Officials from the central government would be present as judges."

"It seems it has all been settled," Kisuke muttered discontentedly.

The mediator cleared his throat. "What does the East say to the proposal?"

Kisuke looked around at his assembled men. Their faces were scared but resolute. He turned back to the mediator. "Since it seems we have no alternative, the East is in agreement. We would, however, like the record to show that we acceded under pressure." He resumed his seat.

The mediator gave a small sigh of relief as he prepared ink and paper for the document. "Would it be possible to choose the contestants this evening? It would expedite the trial. This matter ought to be decided before winter."

"I stand here for the West!" boomed Kakubei. His followers nodded.

"And I for the East," Kurazaemon responded, struggling to rise.

At once Kakubei stepped forward and confronted the old man. "Not you!" he barked. "Kisuke is the one who has argued with us from the first. Why doesn't he step forward as representative?"

The Eastern men gasped at this rudeness. Kisuke hissed savagely, "Have you no respect for an elder of our village?"

"Our quarrel is not with him! Everyone knows the whole dispute would have been settled long ago if not for your pig-headedness, Kisuke!" Kakubei folded his arms, a gesture both impudent and challenging.

The mediator stood and laid a hand on Kisuke's arm, speaking quietly. "If you do not agree, the entire region will fall into discord. You are requested to be the East's representative in the ordeal. Please say yes."

Kisuke bristled and shouted, "I am not afraid! It will be an honor to represent the East. We shall see who is strongest! We shall see who has the grace of the gods!" Immediately the document was drawn up and approved by both sides, whereupon the meeting ended. The mediator and a few selected men from each faction walked to the shrine to consecrate the document and inform the priest of the decision. The mediator then hurried to hire a messenger who would copy the document and take it to Edo.

That night, Kisuke and Kurazaemon sat on Kisuke's verandah with a jug of cold sake and a tobacco box between them, bathed in the light of the enormous full moon. From inside the house came the piping voices of children and the flump of futons being laid out for bedtime. Both men's hearts were heavy, and the dear sights and sounds of ordinary life were not enough to cheer them.

The old man broke the silence. "Well, I tried. You heard me. I tried."

"Kurazaemon, you have nothing to apologize for. You were right as an elder of the village to offer yourself for the ordeal, and the West was right to insist that I should be the one. It all ended as it was supposed to."

"Yes, perhaps. Still, it should have been me. I am old. If I failed, I would leave no family behind in disgrace." Both men knew that whoever failed would be immediately executed. It was the ancient custom, inextricably linked to the ordeal.

Kurazaemon got to his feet. "Well, you have some time to prepare. The government officials certainly won't be here before autumn. You must tell your family, and perform some cleansing rituals. I'm sure the priest of the shrine will know just what is required." The old man called out a few words of thanks to Kisuke's wife and took his leave.

Kisuke sat silent a few minutes, then called his wife. "O-mae! Come here and sit down a moment with me. Bring my mother."

Admonishing the children to be quiet and stay in bed, Kisuke's wife brought his mother, Ume, and both women sat down on the old boards of the verandah.

Kisuke turned his body to face them directly and sat in the formal posture, his legs folded under him. "A decision has been made. The land dispute will be decided in a trial by fire. I have agreed to represent the Eastern faction in this trial. For this, I will need your help. Please assist me to acquit myself honorably." He made a deep bow.

At this dire formality, both women turned white with fear. The old lady recovered first. "We will do everything in our power to help you win the day. We realize that the honor of our family and the entire Eastern faction is at stake." The women bowed, and Kisuke dismissed them. He slowly filled and lit his *kiseru* pipe, and sat watching the curling smoke rise in the moonlight for a long time.

August 14, 1619

The screech of cicadas seemed to tighten and intensify the glaring sunshine. Outside Kisuke's big house, the world was hot, bright, and loud; inside, it was as cool and dark as a cave. Kisuke sat on the straw mat in front of the family altar, fanning himself with a round, stiff paper fan and resting his eyes on the smooth untroubled face of the bronze Amida Buddha statue in the main niche. The altar was crowded with fruit, flowers, candles, and sweets. It was the O-Bon holiday, the day of the dead. The ancestor spirits were here for their annual visit.

Help me to do what I must do, he petitioned them silently.

There were footsteps in the entranceway, and a voice called out. The women scurried to receive the visitors. Kisuke looked up as two men, his relatives, entered the room. They took their seats on the cushions his wife set out, and made small talk until cool glasses of tea were brought and the wife withdrew. Then one of them placed a bundle wrapped in white cloth before Kisuke, and bowed. "It is ready. I have brought it."

Kisuke returned the bow and unfolded the cloth to reveal a large, black iron ax. He hefted it in his hands, feeling its weight and roughness. "It is well done."

"The craftsman guarantees that the weight and size are according to the government decree."

"What about the Western faction? Is their ax ready?"

"I believe so. They have their own craftsman." Kisuke knew this. The headquarters of the Western faction, the "ironmaster's village," was famous for metalwork. He suspected that this was one reason why Kakubei had insisted on this particular kind of trial by fire.

"Thank you for your trouble." Kisuke bowed the men out, and after they left, placed the ax reverently before the family altar. It would remain there until it was brought to Watamuki shrine on the day of the trial.

Kisuke looked at the ax and imagined it glowing with heat. He looked at his hands and imagined them smoking, red and black with burns. A shiver passed through him. Then he imagined the ax lying on the shrine altar, branding the wood with its heat, showing his success. He would do it. He would.

"Kisuke-san?" His mother, Ume, opened the reed screen and approached him. "The ax is ready?"

"Yes." He gestured to the baleful thing lying in front of the altar. She came close and examined it without touching it. Then she turned to him. "How about you—are you ready?"

"I will be." He didn't look at her. "The shrine priest will meet

34

with me for spiritual counsel every five days until the ordeal. The night before, I will perform a vigil at the shrine."

"When do you think it will be?"

"There is no word yet from Edo, but we expect a messenger any day now. It will certainly be before the cold weather."

"My son, look at me." He raised his eyes to her shrewd old ones. "You must not fail. Do you hear me? You must not fail."

"I know."

She looked at him even more intensely. "If you do fail, you know what my duty will be."

"I'm sure the government officials will arrange for immediate execution according to custom. The Western faction stipulated that."

"Even so." Her eyes bored into him, and he understood her meaning.

October 18, 1619

The day of the trial by fire dawned bright and crisp. A fine white ground mist was already dissipating in the mild warmth of the rising sun. The tall cypresses looked down on the shrine, absolutely motionless, their dark depths pierced with slanting sunbeams.

Kisuke, dressed in formal white, the cold iron ax grasped in his hands, stood on the broad grassy strip just inside the big stone *torii* gate. Opposite him, similarly attired and holding his own ax, was Kakubei. The members of each faction were gathered behind their champions. The priest had made his preparations while it was still dark, and now stood to attention at the side. All was in readiness, and they waited only for the arrival of the government officials.

Kisuke stood still, breathing the scent of the olive flowers. Out of the corner of his eye, he saw a form outside the gate, twenty paces or so down the road. His mother, clad in ceremonial white like the rest, stood there motionless, holding her long-staffed *naginata* halberd. She had said farewell to Kisuke the previous night, just before he left for the shrine, both of them sitting facing the family altar. Now all her tears had been shed, and she was ready to do her duty—to cut down her son if he should lose the contest. She was determined to save the family the shame of a public execution.

There was a stir at the end of the road, and the official party came in sight, their gorgeous court clothes glinting in the level rays of the sunrise. Tall standards bearing the Tokugawa crest were carried on poles at the front. Twenty or so lesser nobles from the shogunate in Edo, along with local officials who would act as witnesses, walked behind the three horses bearing the government-appointed judges, all in silence. They passed Kisuke's mother without a glance.

A few of the men from both factions, including Kurazaemon, had been invited to the billet of the officials the previous night, and had drunk with them, but this morning was all business. The officials reined in their horses and dismounted. The creak and jingle of the tack was very loud in the stillness. Then the three walked smoothly through the gate in single file and up the gravel path between the waiting villagers. The priest followed them, gesturing to Kisuke and Kakubei to follow.

The two rivals walked side by side up the gravel path, their straw sandals whispering, their white clothes rustling. Kisuke could hear Kakubei breathing heavily. Was he excited, or scared? Thanks to his training at the hands of the shrine priest, Kisuke himself was calm, though one corner of his mind was crying out in terror. As they came to the shrine building, where the altar was visible in the dimness at the top of a short flight of wooden steps, Kisuke noticed that a large dais had been set up to one side. This was where the officials would sit. Directly before the altar building were two large charcoal braziers filled with glowing coals, their heat making the air shiver above them. Wooden signs with the legends "East" and "West" had been erected before the braziers, and two buckets, made of fresh pine wood and filled with water, stood next to them on the gravel. Draped over each bucket was a thin straw mat about the size of a piece of scroll paper. The braziers were attended by two shrine assistants.

After the judges were seated on the dais, the priest gave the signal for two *miko* dancers to perform the rites of purification. They danced in the slanting sunshine, with capes of crisp white lawn overlaying under-kimono of a startling red, their faces painted celadon white, the glinting ceremonial bells held in their upraised hands, turning in slow circles on the green turf. Kisuke had never seen anything so beautiful. If this was to be his last day on earth, he was grateful for such a sight to close his life. The ritual ended, and the dancers withdrew.

The moment had arrived. The judge in the center spoke. "Let the axes be placed upon the braziers."

Kisuke and Kakubei approached their respective braziers and laid the iron axes in the beds of coals. A few orange sparks spiraled up lazily. During the pause while the axes heated up, one of the noblemen opened a scroll and read out the proclamation in measured tones.

"Hear ye all! Officials of Edo, noblemen of this region, heads of villages, we are gathered here to witness the contest of Kisuke of the Eastern faction and Kakubei of the Western faction, who will endure the Ordeal of Fire and Iron to win the rights to Mount

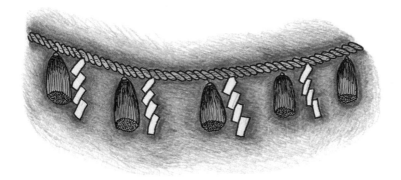

Toyama and adjoining peaks. Everything is prepared and now the ordeal will be performed. The two contestants will approach the braziers at the same time and dip their hands in the water for purification. Then they will receive the straw mats, which will be placed on the palms of their bare hands, and upon them the red-hot axes. They will walk ten steps—five steps on the ground and five steps on the wooden stairs. They will lay the axes on the altar in front of the sacred sake and the sacred leaves, reflected in the sacred mirror overhead. The one who completes this task, or comes closest to completing it, will be deemed the winner and his faction will be awarded the rights to the mountain range. The loser will be executed tomorrow. The Shogun has spoken!"

Dead silence, broken only by the whisper of the burning coals. Kisuke braced himself for the command to go forward. At this moment, however, the three judges were seen to confer among themselves. Then the judge in the center gestured to the one reading the proclamation and whispered in his ear. The nobleman cleared his throat and resumed.

"Herewith a codicil. It is the will of the Shogun that the two contestants will exchange axes. The Western representative will carry the Eastern ax and the Eastern representative will carry the Western ax."

In spite of the solemnity of the occasion, the onlookers gasped softly at this turn of events. Kisuke could not imagine what this might mean. He heard a small sound, like a squeak, escape Kakubei.

"Begin!"

The two contestants walked forward together. Before the braziers, they dipped their hands in the cool water and accepted the straw mats, holding them like trays with their hands underneath. As ordered, they changed places so each faced the brazier of the other's faction. Both men stretched their hands out over the beds of coals. Water from them dripped and hissed with small jets of steam.

The assistants raised the glowing red axes with heavy iron tongs. With a loud shout of self-encouragement, Kisuke received the ax on his mat, which immediately began to burn, yellow flames licking between his fingers. Still yelling as loudly as he could, he took five quick steps toward the shrine. The mat was burned away by the time he began to climb the steps, and when he reached the altar, he had to shake his hands to rid them of the ax, which had adhered to his skin. It fell with a thump to the altar and a tail of smoke arose as it branded itself into the wood. Panting, he brought his ruined palms together as best he could and bowed to the altar.

It was only after Kisuke had turned around that he was able to notice what had happened to his rival. Kakubei had fallen to his knees on the gravel before the braziers, screaming hoarsely, cowering and pressing his hands under his armpits. The red hot ax lay before him on the ground, along with the remains of the straw mat, still in flames. Even in his extremity, Kisuke felt Kakubei's disgrace. He had not taken even one step, and now his life was forfeit. What were all his proud words worth?

Members of the official party now came forward and grasped Kakubei by the arms, holding him between them. The dishonored man stood trembling, his streaming eyes fixed on the ground. Meanwhile two other officials led Kisuke back to the bucket of water, and he plunged his hands into it with a cry of relief.

The central judge raised his voice to speak over the muted babble of the crowd. "I have officially witnessed the events of this trial. I declare the East the winner in the dispute. The representative of the West will meet his death tomorrow at the execution stage of Hibari-no. This trial is now concluded."

The men of the East could barely contain themselves till the officials and the priest had withdrawn to a nearby shrine building for refreshments. Then they crowded around Kisuke, bringing bandages and liniment for his poor hands and all talking at once, showering him with congratulations. Straightening to his full height for a moment, Kisuke looked around until his eyes found the unhappy Kakubei being led away by the officials. Kakubei took one look over his shoulder and met Kisuke's eyes, then walked with bowed head, sobbing softly in the agony of his disgrace. His men fell in behind him silently.

Later that night, there was feasting and jollity in the villages of the Eastern faction as the autumn night closed in. Jubilant shouts and excited chatter arose from knots of people milling in the narrow lanes. Children swooped and scurried underfoot, feeling the triumph without understanding it. Every house was brightly lit, and the brightest of all was Kisuke's.

The largest room was filled with the scent of sake and food and the happy chatting of twenty or thirty drinking men seated at the low tables. Village women hovered behind them, replacing each sake bottle the instant it was emptied. At the head of the table, nearest the family altar, Kisuke sat with the Amida Buddha staring peaceably over his shoulder. His hands were white-wrapped paws, but he still got plenty to drink, because every time a grateful villager knelt beside him with sake bottle poised to pour him a toast, his mother, who sat next to him, accepted the toast and held the small ceramic cup to her son's lips.

Kisuke felt dazed. The day had been full of pain, official documents, pain, congratulations from relatives and neighbors, pain, pain and more pain. He was exhausted from enduring it, but the sake helped a little. When he surfaced for a few moments, he had time to wonder about the strange command of the judge. Why had the shogun commanded them to exchange axes before the trial? Had he been told something? Was the ax he had carried identical to the one he had kept in his house for two months? He couldn't remember noticing any difference, but then, his agony during the ordeal would have prevented that.

After the speeches and toasts were concluded and everyone was conversing, old Kurazaemon sat stiffly down beside Kisuke. He raised the cup he was holding and received a measure of sake from the old lady. "Here's to you, my friend," he said and downed it in a gulp. Ume helped Kisuke return the toast, then tactfully shuffled back a few inches so that the two men could converse.

The old man looked Kisuke in the face for the first time. He saw tears squeezing out of his friend's eyes and wandering down his sake-reddened cheeks. "Is it very bad?" he said in a low voice.

"I won, Kurazaemon. That is the important thing. I won the contest and the mountain is safe." After a pause, he added, "That was a strange command, there at the end. The command to exchange axes. Why do you suppose they did that?"

"Actually, I heard something, and I want to tell you about it. But it's a secret, and mind you keep it. It could mean both our heads if it were found out. Your victory would be taken away from you and they might have to hold another trial."

Kisuke was aghast. For a moment his pain ceased. He felt as if he were falling down a well. "What is it?"

"The Western faction cheated. Their ax was made with a hollow center so that it would weigh less and the iron would cool faster. They say it was all Kakubei's idea. He had a notion to win easily and he convinced the ironmasters to make a lighter ax."

Kisuke could not say a word. The enormity of this sacrilege took his breath away. He understood that Kakubei, a stranger, was an unknown quantity, but the other members of the Western faction—what could have possessed them to go along with such a dangerous fraud? And it was true what Kurazaemon said. If this secret got out, Kisuke's own victory would be called into question, since it was the cheating ax he had carried. It would have to remain a dire secret, carried by him and Kurazaemon to their graves. He wondered how many other people knew. Might the secret be leaked by someone else? If so, there would certainly be repercussions from the central government.

Kurazaemon, who had been watching his face, nodded slowly. "We can keep the secret, and we must, for the sake of the entire Eastern faction."

The insistent throb was returning to Kisuke's hands. He knew he must drink a lot more, otherwise he wouldn't be able to sleep. He signaled with a jerk of his head, and Ume at once came forward and proffered the sake bottle to Kurazaemon. After downing his toast as it was held to his lips by Ume, he said, "Drink with me, my friend. The mountain is ours forever. No one can take it away."

It was only much later, lying in his futon watching the dawn break, that the final question arose in Kisuke's mind.

Had the judge known? And how had he known?

Author's note: This is a true story. In October 1619, a trial like the one described was won by my husband's ancestor Kisuke, over his opponent Kakubei. It is the most famous "trial by fire" of the period, and is chronicled in the book "Gamo Gunshi" (History of the Gamo Area). To this day, every year on October 18, two members of our family attend a commemoration ceremony at Watamuki Shrine in Nishioji, Hino Township. The ceremony is called Tekka Matsuri, or Festival of Iron and Fire.

Love and Duty

Wednesday

"Excuse me, Joanne-sensei. A moment please?"

Joanne looked up from the gray metal desk piled with the English grammar workbooks she was correcting. Standing there, fiddling with an empty teacup, was a woman she knew by sight, a painfully thin math teacher who occupied a similar desk halfway down the long teachers' room.

"Yes," the woman continued, "this is the first time we are speaking, I think. My name is Kikuchi. Nice to meet you."

"Nice to meet you too," answered Joanne. Sounds like my English textbook, she thought.

"Actually, I have a favor to ask."

"Yes?"

"Well, you know it is Valentine's Day this weekend . . ." Joanne nodded. How could anyone miss the huge red and pink displays of chocolate, shelf upon shelf, front and center at every supermarket? Disney chocolate, soccer chocolate, whiskey chocolate. Chocolate golf balls and chocolate sports cars, chocolate wrapped in seductive gold and red like the whorehouse in *Gone with the Wind*. Joanne was glad that at least she hadn't heard any 'official' Valentine's Day songs . . . so far. It was only a matter of time before shoppers got treated to "That's Amore," or some even more excruciating selection, on store Muzak from January 5 till February 13. Suppressing a sigh, she turned her attention back to her colleague.

"I was wondering, would you mind giving a gift of chocolate to my son? He is in the first grade and I just know he would be overjoyed to receive chocolate from an American." Ms. Kikuchi gave a small, nervous, closed-mouth smile.

Huh? thought Joanne. She didn't know this woman and she certainly didn't know her son. Besides, she had always considered the Japanese Valentine's Day traditions weird in the extreme. But Ms. Kikuchi was waiting for an answer.

"Um, can I let you know? Excuse me—I have to return these workbooks after the lunch break." Joanne knew a fellow teacher would acknowledge that work took precedence.

"Oh, certainly. Sorry to disturb you. You are so busy." Having, with no irony whatsoever, awarded Joanne the coveted Medal of Being Very Busy, Ms. Kikuchi moved away, still cradling her teacup. Joanne turned back to her task.

On her way home from the high school that evening, swaying from a hanging strap in the train, Joanne went over the conversation in her mind. So many things about it annoyed her. First, although a stranger, Ms. Kikuchi had used her first name. *Joanne-sensei*. Joanne knew it was common practice for foreign English teachers to be called by their given names instead of their surnames, even though no one would think of calling a Japanese teacher by her given name—probably no one would even know it. As a matter of fact, Joanne happened to have a perfectly good Japanese surname. It was Nozaki. She had been married for ten years to a Japanese man and they had two children. So how come she wasn't Nozaki-sensei to the teachers she worked with? Even her students called her Joanne-sensei. *I can't get no respect*, she whispered to herself.

But that wasn't all. (Joanne noticed a group of school kids giggling at her and angled them out of her line of vision.) Ms. Kikuchi had tried to co-opt her into a ritual that was ostensibly based on a Western holiday, but was in fact completely Japanese. How thoughtless was that? What did Japanese people know about Valentine's Day? They had *women* giving chocolate to *men*, for heaven's sake. Joanne sighed. She knew, she remembered, what the day was really about. The fluttery anticipation of wondering what one's boyfriend or husband had in mind for the day, the roses, the candlelight, the soft music. Valentine's Day was about love. *Romantic* love! In Japan it had been made into yet another social obligation. Plus, how come Joanne, a grown woman, was being asked to give chocolate to some unknown first-grade boy? The whole thing was ridiculous.

By the time she turned the key in her front door, Joanne was fuming.

Saeko had many names, many titles. She was "O-mae" to her husband, "Mama" to her son, "Oku-san" to her neighbors, and "Kikuchi-

sensei" to her students. The last person to call her by her first name had been her mother, now two years deceased. "Saeko-chan," her mother had said in her last illness. "Please make sure everything is properly prepared for the funeral. Don't sit here with me; you should be cleaning the house. Please check the dishes and utensils to see nothing is missing." And she had.

Thinking about the past, she stepped blindly off the curb. "Oku-san! Be careful!" shouted a nearby shopkeeper, and a car brake screeched. Saeko gasped and pulled up short. A moment later, with a hasty "Sorry" to the shopkeeper, she walked on down the busy, twilit neighborhood street. The memory of her mother gave way to a fast-motion parade of other thoughts and concerns, which accompanied her like importunate children as she hurried along.

She thought about taking out the garbage that morning. This morning, one of her neighbors had been on garbage detail, standing next to the collection area to make sure everyone brought their bags out on time. It was Saeko's turn to do this next week, but she wasn't sure if she could stand there till eight o'clock and still be on time for work. And, speaking of time, did she have time to stop at the market now? Probably not. Tomorrow, then.

Her thoughts jumped to a different topic. Her husband Masato had telephoned her from work, saying that he needed an envelope of money for a company funeral tomorrow. Was there enough cash in the house? How about his black suit? She would have to get it ready this evening. And she needed to talk to him about her mother's three-year memorial service, which must be scheduled some time next month. How many guests would there be, and what kind of take-home gifts should she arrange for them?

Another jump. Work today. One of her second-year students had been asleep almost the entire lesson. This wasn't the first time, either. Should she contact his parents? Perhaps he stayed up late studying or went to cram school till ten in the evening, as she knew many of the students did. But what if he was hanging around behind the convenience store late at night, smoking (or worse) with *some bad kids? Did his hair look any longer than usual, were his pants any baggier than usual? Saeko knew it was part of her job to be observant about these things, but these days she couldn't seem to concentrate.*

Now the exchange with Joanne-sensei circled back to the top of her brain. It had taken most of her courage to approach the foreigner. But she needed lots of Valentine chocolate for Kenji-kun this year. She hoped Joanne-sensei would agree to her request and provide something really special.

It was full dark when Saeko approached the after-hours center annexed to the primary school. She peeked in the brightly lighted window before pushing open the door. Kenji was there, roughhousing around the room, brandishing what looked like a plastic baseball bat. As usual, he was one of the last children to be picked up. The teacher sitting in the corner looked tired. Saeko prepared her apology as she went in.

"I'm home!"

The unmistakable thuds of briefcase and shoes sounded on the entryway floor, and then Hiroyuki came into the kitchen, loosening his tie. Busy at the sink, Joanne raised her cheek for his kiss. "Hi, how are you?"

"Okay. Tired. Where are the kids?"

"In their rooms doing their homework, I hope." As she spoke, Joanne heard the upstairs bedroom doors slide open and slam against their tracks, then the elephant stampede as Megumi and Taro took the stairs two at a time to greet Daddy. The little kitchen was suddenly full of noise and love. A flurry of combined English and Japanese rose on the air, mingling with the aromatic steam of the curry stew as Joanne lifted the lid to give it a final stir. "Okay, everyone, wash your hands! Dinner's ready!" Hiroyuki was pulled out of the room by his children, who grabbed his hands, one on each side. Joanne put the finishing touches on the meal. The "evening zoo" had begun. She didn't mind it—her family were her joy, and she relished the happy noise and confusion of a group of people who were at ease with each other. It was a welcome contrast to her workday.

A couple of hours later, dinner, baths, and bedtime stories completed, Joanne sat opposite Hiroyuki on the floor at the low *kotatsu* table. The house rang with the kind of silence that follows a sustained period of loud noise. She knew they both relished that silence—which was why, unlike most couples, they left the TV off in the evening—but she needed to break it tonight.

"Something weird happened at school today. Can I tell you about it?"

"What?" Hiroyuki's eyes didn't leave his newspaper.

"One of the teachers asked me to give a *giri-choco* to her six-year-old son." Joanne used the term "duty chocolate," which was a universally accepted Valentine's Day social custom in Japan. She herself had been the indirect recipient of a lot of giri-choco over the years—Hiroyuki always brought home the chocolate he received from the "office ladies." She knew they didn't have romantic designs on Hiroyuki; they just bought into the meaningless gesture—women give chocolate to men—like millions of others. And like most men, Hiroyuki didn't like chocolate that much.

Joanne gave the back of the paper a flick with her finger. "Hey. This is important."

"Okay." He laid the paper down and looked at her.

"What did I just say?" she asked, teasing.

"Something about giri-choco. I was listening."

"Humph. Well, it's a wonder. Anyway, what do you think? This teacher I barely know asked me to give her son a chocolate gift for Valentine's Day."

"Kind of weird, you're right. Still, it's only giri-choco. Why not do it?"

"Because that's not what Valentine's Day is all about!"

He looked at her quizzically. "Do you mean to tell me Valentine's Day isn't about giri-choco?"

"Oh you! I'll giri-choco you, with my fist!" Launching an attack with her father's favorite phrase, she got him in a good-natured headlock and a moment later they were on the floor in each other's arms.

"While we're on the subject, what are *we* doing for Valentine's Day this year?" Hiroyuki asked, his mouth in her hair.

Joanne knew this was as much "learned behavior" as her own habit of bowing when answering the telephone, but she was grateful to him for making the effort. She knew a lot of her friends' husbands didn't do things like remembering Valentine's Day, preferring to stand on their Japanese male dignity. Though born and raised in Japan, Hiroyuki had the advantage not only of their ten-year marriage, but a long stint as an exchange student in the United States in his university days. Thank goodness for a bit of Westernization, Joanne thought. It had made all the difference to their relationship.

"Dinner out!" she responded excitedly. "A family dinner at Tony Roma's. Plenty of Surf 'n'Turf, a big dessert. Sunday night!"

"You got it." Hiroyuki stood up and held out his hand. "Coming to bed?"

"Mama!" shouted Kenji as soon as he saw her. He dropped the bat and rushed at her, almost knocking her off her feet with his exuberant greeting. Saeko laughed and glanced at the teacher in charge. "I'm sorry," she said, disentangling herself from her son. "I'll try to get here earlier next time. I realize you want to get home after your hard day." She gathered up Kenji's belongings and buttoned up his coat.

Mother and son walked home through the winter darkness. Kenji held her hand, swinging her arm up and down, chattering about the events of his day. Saeko listened fondly. She envied her son his boundless energy and enthusiasm.

"Do you know what day it is on Saturday?" she asked him.

"Valentine's Day!" he crowed. "Chocolate!"

"Yes, chocolate, and I'm sure you're going to get a lot. My big handsome boy! All the girls will want to give you chocolate."

"Yay!"

"And I'll tell you something else, something nice."

"Oh, Mama, what is it? Tell me!"

"Well, you know there is a foreigner working in Mama's school, and you just might get some chocolate from her as well. It's sure to be special, because she is American. Maybe even with a note in English just for you." Kenji jumped up and down with glee. Saeko smiled to herself at the thought of him opening chocolate from a foreigner. If only Joanne-sensei would say yes!

They arrived home, and Kenji turned on the TV, while Saeko went into the kitchen and sat down at the table. After a few minutes she got up, returning with a glass of water. Masato would be late, as he was every night, and she began to go over the details of the two dinners she had arranged. Curry rice for Kenji, then an assortment of snacks and beer for Masato followed by grilled fish, soup and rice. How the hours would drag by until he came home at eleven o'clock! Even then, she would have to wait until he had finished eating and watching the late news on TV and taking his bath, before she could get in the bath herself and go to sleep.

Saeko pushed herself up from the table, went to the refrigerator and took out the pot of curry she had made that morning.

Thursday

Joanne had such a good time with Hiroyuki laughing about giri-choco that she almost forgot about Ms. Kikuchi. However, the next morning, there she was again at Joanne's elbow as she prepared for her first class. This time, Ms. Kikuchi ceremoniously set down a fresh cup of tea before her.

"Good morning, Joanne-sensei. Have you, perhaps, considered my request?"

"Ah, good morning." Joanne launched into the response she had decided on. "Well, Kikuchi-sensei, you may not realize it, but we Americans view Valentine's Day a bit differently from Japanese people. For us it is a romantic holiday between adults, and has nothing to do with children." She pushed aside a dim memory of exchanging cards with corny sayings in her third-grade class back in Peoria, Illinois, circa 1992. That wasn't *real* Valentine's Day, she told herself.

Ms. Kikuchi was not at all flustered. She looked exactly like any Japanese person receiving the news that Christmas was actually not about eating strawberry shortcake, but about the birth of Jesus. Her look said, *Yes, but this is Japan.*

"Ah, is that right?" she said vaguely. "Still, I'm sure you wouldn't mind making a little boy happy. Anything would do. Please?"

"I'm sorry. I can't. Please forgive me." Joanne rushed off as the bell rang, leaving the tea undrunk and Ms. Kikuchi standing.

On a brisk tour through the supermarket that evening, Joanne found herself thinking about Ms. Kikuchi again, and felt something that she hadn't felt since those first difficult years in Japan—the excruciating, thin-skinned sensitivity of being a foreigner. Why were these people so everlastingly polite and considerate to one another, and so willfully clueless when it came to foreigners? Joanne knew that her sensitivity was just as ridiculous as their thoughtlessness—but oh, there were so MANY of them and only one of her! She wanted, longed, to just be herself, but it was an uphill battle. Everyone around her seemed to be silently bellowing, "Resistance is useless! You will be a buffoon for the Japanese and do your part to maintain the comfort level of our society. And you will LIKE IT!" Why did it seem as though Ms. Kikuchi was singling her out? Had she made the same request of any of the Japanese teachers at the high school? Why did these people seem to want foreigners to participate in whatever ridiculous thing they came up with? *Do it yourselves, but leave me out of it!* she wanted to scream. I AM NOT ONE OF YOU!

"More."

Masato held up his empty rice bowl without looking away from the TV. Saeko took it and refilled it from the rice cooker stationed at her elbow. As her husband ate, she tried to concentrate on the lesson plan for the next day, which she had opened surreptitiously on the other side of the kotatsu. But she kept thinking about Joanne-sensei. She had never spoken to a foreigner before, and this was her first experience of the devastating directness she had heard about. Joanne-sensei's refusal was incomprehensible. How could anyone just say no when asked to do something? Especially a woman? She tried to remember if she had ever done such a thing. Her own mother had set an example of selfless womanhood, right up to the end. That was how women were supposed to be. It was a woman's job to keep the wheels of society turning smoothly, as it was a man's job to keep the money coming in. Were foreigners really so fundamentally different?

"I'm done." Masato clattered his chopsticks down on the table, pointed the remote at the TV, and rose. "Dinner tonight was better than last night."

"I'm glad you liked it, now how about a bath?" Saeko responded.

"I think I might be catching a cold. I'll skip my bath for once. You go ahead, I'm going to bed. Good night."

Ten minutes later, Saeko lowered herself gratefully into the steaming water and closed her eyes. As she did so, a wonderful idea occurred to her. She knew what would convince Joanne-sensei to give Kenji the chocolate. Tomorrow morning before school, she would sit Kenji down and have him write a letter, maybe with some of his cute drawings. No one could resist a letter written by a child!

Saeko dried herself and put on her nightgown, averting her eyes from the mirror.

Friday

The next morning, when Joanne came to work, she saw a white envelope carefully positioned in the middle of her desk. Feeling like a submarine officer upping periscope, she raised her head cautiously and glanced down the row of teachers' desks, each with its occupant busy getting ready for the school day. Ms. Kikuchi was there, but she seemed to be searching through a drawer, her head almost invisible.

Joanne angled herself so her back was turned directly to Ms. Kikuchi, and picked up the envelope. No markings of any kind. Inside, she found a folded piece of white paper, which when unfolded showed the large, wobbly pencil printing of a small child. In Japanese, it said, "Please give me chocolate, Sensei!" It was signed "Kikuchi Kenji" and surrounded by drawings of flying KitKat bars.

Oh boy, thought Joanne. She's raised the stakes. And I know what I have to do now. It's something I should have done right at the beginning.

Leaving the note on her desk, Joanne stood up, walked straight to the principal's office at the end of the teachers' room, and knocked on the door. Hearing a muffled grunt of acknowledgment, she went in.

"Good morning, Joanne-sensei."

Don't let it get to you, she told herself. "Principal-sensei, may I please have a moment?"

"Yes?" Principal Goto was a large, heavyset middle-aged man. Though he had a kind face, his bulk was intimidating. Joanne found it a little hard to know where to begin.

"I'm afraid I have to complain about the inappropriate behavior of one of my fellow teachers," she finally said, and briefly recounted Ms. Kikuchi's escalating requests over the past three days.

Principal Goto regarded her for a moment. "In what way do you regard this as inappropriate? Was Kikuchi rude or insulting to you?"

In spite of over a decade of schooling herself in the ways of this country, Joanne felt her anger growing. Her eyes snapped. "Principal-sensei, I am a Westerner. We have certain ideas about these holidays that are different from Japanese people's, and I don't feel I should be forced to participate in your rituals."

"Did you explain this to her?"

"Yes, I did, but she doesn't seem to understand. I came to you because I resent being bothered in the workplace with something I regard as a personal request. Kikuchi-sensei is taking advantage of her status as my colleague to get something from me." As Joanne spoke, she saw Principal Goto's eyes glaze over. She knew he was about to take refuge in platitudes.

"You know, Joanne-sensei, my job as principal is to promote the smooth running of the school for everyone's benefit. The teachers need to teach and the students need to learn. Anything that disrupts this should come to my notice. Is Kikuchi's request preventing you from doing your job?"

"No," Joanne admitted. "But I have been disturbed by it, and since it happened at work, I felt I should come to you."

"Well, I suppose I could talk to her. Tell her how you feel. I'm not sure what her reaction will be, since it is evident she doesn't think she is guilty of any wrongdoing. Would you prefer to be present?"

"No, that's all right. Thank you for your time." Feeling that she had accomplished as much as could be expected, Joanne withdrew.

She's seen the letter, thought Saeko, peering between the stacked books on her desk toward Joanne-sensei. Now she's opening it. Now she's . . . With a gasp of dismay, she watched the other woman straighten up and march straight to the principal's office. Surely this didn't have anything to do with her, or with the letter! Her heart raced as she collected her teaching materials in preparation for the first class. Out of the corner of her eye, she saw Joanne-sensei come out, her heels tapping angrily, and sail out the door leading to the classrooms without a glance in her direction. No question. The visit to the principal had definitely been about her.

Saeko's mind raced. Would she lose her job? She had heard of such things happening after contretemps with foreign teachers. She had to keep working, had to keep saving, for Kenji's sake. There was so little time left. But the principal would never understand. How could Joanne-sensei have caused so much trouble, so casually? Terrible visions chased each other around in her head, and big black blobs began to obscure her vision. Not now! She breathed deeply.

"Excuse me, Kikuchi-sensei," the secretary approached her. "Would you mind stepping into Principal-sensei's office for a moment?" Summoning all her strength, Saeko smiled at the secretary. "Certainly," she whispered. She felt the stinging darts of the other teachers' curious gazes on her back as she knocked and entered.

"Good morning, Principal-sensei. You wished to see me?"

"Yes," Principal Goto harrumphed. "I'm sorry to disturb you just before class, but I just had a visit from Joanne-sensei. She says you have been asking her to give Valentine's Day chocolate to your son. She seems upset by this request. I'm not sure where I come into it, but . . ."

Saeko was aghast. To bother the principal with such a thing! Scarlet shame chased pale fear across her face. "I don't know what to say, Principal-sensei. I had no idea she would get so upset. It is all my fault. I implore you to let the matter drop."

"Well, that's what I would like to do, but you know, I must keep everyone happy, and that includes the foreign employees. Would you mind offering her an apology?"

"Yes, of course I will apologize to her. Principal-sensei, I am so ashamed. Please forget you ever heard about this matter. You have nothing to worry about."

Principal Goto's face relaxed with relief. His Japanese sensibility told him that an apology would fix everything. "Now, we must all get to work. Nothing further needs to be said about this. Good day."

Saeko never knew how she got out of the principal's room.

To avoid an unpleasant scene, Joanne dashed to her first class as soon as her interview with Principal Goto was over. She felt a little wobbly after bearding the principal in his den, but the routine of work had a calming effect. At lunchtime, she returned to her desk and took her sandwich out of her bag. The other teachers seemed quieter than usual, and that was kind of peaceful. She ate her lunch, reading a book at the same time, and went to her afternoon classes without encountering Ms. Kikuchi. So far, so good. Maybe Principal Goto's little talk had done the trick. In any case, Valentine's Day was tomorrow, and there was no school, so that was the end of the Tale of the Math Teacher and her Greedy Chocolate-Loving Son.

As Joanne was about to leave for the day, the secretary approached her desk holding a large white card. "Excuse me, Joanne-sensei, would you like to sign this?"

Joanne flicked her eyes toward the card. It was a *shikishi*, a traditional group message card, and seemed already to have about twenty messages written on it. Unlike other shikishi Joanne had seen, this one was pure white and all the messages were written in black. "Uh, what's this for?"

"One of the teachers was taken ill this morning and is now in the Dai-ichi Hospital in critical condition. We are sending her a get-well message."

Joanne fumbled for a black pen. "That is terrible. Which teacher was it?"

"The math teacher, Kikuchi-sensei."

Saeko was swimming in dark brown depths. She felt large and soft, warm and peaceful. Then a light appeared, floating toward her through the murk. As it approached she felt herself shrink and dwindle into something more like her usual small, hard, conscious self. She opened her eyes. Everything was white, not brown. Drifting in the white was a tan-colored blob that gradually resolved itself into the top half of a face she didn't know. The bottom half was obscured by a surgical mask.

"So, Kikuchi-san, you are awake. That's good. I am Dr. Masashi and you are in the Dai-Ichi Hospital."

"Hospital?" Saeko murmured. All the secrecy and pain of the past several months returned in a rush. She felt tears of shame gather in her eyes. "Did you find it?"

"The tumor? We certainly did. Everyone was surprised it was so large! How long have you been hiding it?"

"I knew I didn't have much time left," Saeko said brokenly. "I didn't want to spend my last months on earth in a hospital, wasting money, causing trouble to everyone, causing grief to my husband and my son. I wanted everything to be nice for them, right up to the end."

The doctor blinked. "End? What end? We took the tumor out. It was benign. Everything is fine now. You just need to rest. You are exhausted and underfed, as well as being ill. You women always take too much on yourselves! Why, I wonder." His eyes twinkled, and he left the room.

Saeko closed her eyes and snuggled down in the bed with a huge sigh. Why do we women do what we do? Don't you know, Doctor? Don't you know, my husband? Kenji? Joanne-sensei?

Because of love. It's all about love.

Later, when Saeko next left the dark brown place for the white place, she noticed a patch of red in the middle of her field of vision. She focused gradually on the nightstand beside her. There sat a KitKat bar, topped with a miniature red bow, and a small note in English.

"To Kenji: Happy Valentine's Day from Joanne-sensei."

Saeko smiled sleepily. Her thin white hand went out to the chocolate bar. She carefully removed the little red ribbon and set it aside. Then she unwrapped the KitKat, and ate it down to the last crumb.

The Turtle Stone

1955

Taro was the eldest son of the family who owned the Tsuru-Kame sweetshop. Today he was fifteen years old.

He awoke, as usual, just as dawn was creeping into the small-paned window above his head. He sat up, surrounded by snow-white mounds of warm quilt. Into his nostrils came the scent of woodsmoke from the fires being stoked below, and into his ears came the clack of wooden trays being stacked. Another day at the sweetshop was beginning.

Even though it was his birthday, Taro would not have a party or presents. It was just an ordinary workday for him. He had officially turned fifteen on the previous New Year's Day; according to custom, everyone else in the family also became a year older on that day.

Taro dressed quickly and hurried down the steep wooden stairs to the living room. The round, low table was set for breakfast, and next to it stood a large lacquer rice caddy and a *hibachi* brazier topped with a pot of fragrant, steaming miso soup. As usual, there was no one there. Taro snagged a piece of yellow pickle from the plate on the table and munched it as he stepped through the curtain and down into the kitchen. He stuck his feet into wooden clogs and took a white apron from where it hung on the wall. "Good morning," he called.

"Hurry up!" exclaimed his mother, thrusting a tray of leaf-wrapped *kashiwa-mochi* sweets at him. "Put these into the display case, and get those shutters open." Taro entered seamlessly into the familiar activity of the early morning sweetshop. All around him were wooden tables, his sisters standing at them shaping sweets; wooden steamers piled high over blazing gas jets; dark brown bean paste piled on china plates; his father presiding like a king over all, and his mother, the hardworking queen, inspecting the sweets before they would be presented to the day's customers.

Carrying the rectangular tray, Taro pushed through another curtain into the cool darkness of the shop. He put the tray down on top of the glass display case, opened a sliding door at the front of the shop, and shifted aside one of the heavy wooden shutters as well, in order to step outside. The sun was just coming up, horizontal bars of light shining through the tall cedars of the shrine a hundred yards away. The air was cool and crisp, and he took a big lungful of it. Tiny green leaves decorated every tree in sight. It was full spring, just past festival time, the season of rice

cakes folded in aromatic oak leaves and the cute little rice balls, three on a stick, tinted green, white and pink.

Even though it was so early, the little street was already dotted with shopkeepers, sweeping the paths and throwing ladles of water to lay the dust in front of their shops. Taro called a greeting as he shoved aside the rest of the shutters that covered the shop front and thrust the glass doors wide open. Then he got a glass of water and carried it outside to a huge boulder that stood just outside the shop, on one side of the entrance. This boulder, a natural stone in the shape of a turtle, was the namesake of the shop—Tsuru-Kame, meaning Crane and Turtle, traditional symbols of good luck and longevity. A long life of good work, happy family life, rock-solid business—this was what everyone prayed for. Taro poured the glass of water over the stone and watched it glisten in the sun, his mind aglow with gratitude.

Inside the shop again, he opened the back of the display case and, with a light touch, placed the kashiwa-mochi one by one in rows behind the glass. The white of the rice cakes and the dull green of the oak leaves looked fine against the light wood of the shelf, powdered with a few grains of rice flour. Around him the familiar wooden walls and cabinets looked down, now glowing with coins of sunshine that passed through the tree branches.

Taro worked on, placing the slanted stands at the front and filling them with cellophane bags of colored boiled sweets, lining up the white paper bags of salty rice crackers, interrupting his work every few minutes as fresh trays of sweets were handed out from the kitchen. Lastly he went outside again with the dark-blue split awning curtain, and stretched up to hang it so that the sweets would not be hit with full sunlight. This was the final chore of the early morning, and it signaled that the shop was open for business.

As the sun rose in the sky, the Tsuru-Kame workers took turns snatching a hasty breakfast in between manning the shop or continuing to make sweets, while customers filed in and out. All their meals were taken in this fashion while the shop was open. Glancing up at the loud-ticking clock on the wall, the mother excused herself to prepare lunch—the house kitchen was at the very back of the house, placed so that the ordinary smells of oil and soy sauce and onions wouldn't interfere with the delightful aroma which wafted out into the street, enticing customers to spend an extra coin or two on sweets to brighten their day.

Taro's stint in the shop was almost finished. He rearranged the sweets in the display case neatly, so that the gaps left by previous sales wouldn't show, and thought about lunch. The little shopping street was now crowded, men in work clothes, ladies in striped everyday kimono with big shopping baskets on their arms, the occasional motorcycle or three-wheeled car threading through the people. The constant crowd roiling past the shop was hypnotic, so that Taro had to shake himself when addressed by someone who stood on the other side of the counter. He focused on a quiet, thin man, formally dressed in kimono and *hakama* trousers, and recognized him as the local teacher of the tea ceremony, Yano-sensei. "Yes, sorry, may I help you?"

The teacher smiled. "Hello. May I speak to your father? I wish to order sweets for a tea meeting next week."

Taro bowed low and excused himself. Instead of calling familiarly through the curtain, he walked bodily into the sweets kitchen, approached his father, and spoke in an undertone. This was the way he had been taught to show respect to important customers, or clients, as they were called. The father moved toward the shop curtain, removing his apron.

Taro knew that Yano-sensei was one of their best clients. He always ordered sweets by the dozen before an event, and he always wanted something special. Traditional tea sweets were much more elaborate than the ones sold to passersby, so it was a good opportunity for his father to display his prowess as a sweets maker. He listened from behind the curtain, noting the respectful language exchanged between two men who recognized each other's mastery. He imagined his father carefully writing down the order, making a little sketch of the desired sweet as Yano-sensei described it, his words and movements perfected over generations. One day, he, Taro, would stand there and take orders from important clients. He would be the master.

Taro's mother passed behind him. "Special birthday treat for you with lunch," she whispered. "Go and eat."

1990

Taro stood in the morning sun and poured water over the turtle stone, as he had done almost every day since he was no taller than the boulder himself. Now, however, things were a little different. Five years before, he had installed a small formal garden in front of the shop, with the boulder as its centerpiece. A few reeds, a good-luck *nanten* plant with sprays of white flowers that would later become sprays of red berries, and a white-pebbled miniature path winding through a bed of thick green moss. A knee-high bamboo fence separated this garden from the street.

Taro watched the water run down the stone, then fetched a watering can and wetted down the rest of the garden. The moisture would evaporate quickly in the summer sun, already hot. He felt a little sorry for these plants that had to breathe car exhaust all day, but this was the name of the game now—he had to think of anything that set his shop apart from the others, and enticed the eyes of the tourists who trooped past on their way to the shrine.

He passed into the shop, pushing aside the good old dark-blue awning. There was a small paper with a symbol of a black diamond printed on it, pasted onto the worn wood of the door lintel. It was the sign of mourning—his father had passed away five months ago, as the whole neighborhood knew, and this little paper would stay on the doorway until his father's first-year memorial service rolled around, a subtle message that the shop had been passed on to the next generation.

Taro watched with sharp eyes his own son Shintaro, now twelve years old, who had recently been given the early-morning job of arranging the sweets for the day's custom. Satisfied, he told Shintaro to go get ready for school, and called one of his sisters, now middle-aged, to watch the shop. He had made some changes to the inside, as well. The wooden walls and cabinets were still there, as was the entrance—he had learned, along with the other Commercial Association members, that a traditional façade was just the thing to bring in the tourists—but now the shop was much brighter, thanks to modern lighting, and the display cases were made of brushed aluminum with curved glass fronts. They liked tradition, these tourists, but they also liked a hygienic atmosphere, especially where food was involved. Taro had put a couple of tables and chairs outside under the awning, with a view of the tiny garden, and the shop now served a simple menu of drinks and, in summer, shaved ice. He suddenly remembered the traditional cloth banner reading "Ice" in flamboyant turquoise writing, and hurried to set it up outside. There would be a good trade in shaved ice today, he thought.

This was still very much a family enterprise. Taro ran it with his two elder sisters, whose husbands were salarymen elsewhere in the city. The sisters lived with their own families in separate houses nearby, taking turns helping in the shop. Taro's wife also took a turn—she was a local woman who had grown up visiting the shop, and who did her best, although she wasn't born into a sweets-making family.

Taro returned to the kitchen to check on the production of the day's summer sweets, which were made by pouring sweet-bean-flavored gelatin into small lengths of green bamboo and refrigerating. He now had a couple of young employees, who were skilled enough but required some watching nevertheless. As he bent over inspecting the finished sweets, his sister sidled up to him and said quietly, "Yano-sensei is here."

Taro flung off his apron and bustled into the shop to see the tea teacher, a slight, quiet old man, dressed formally as usual, standing before the counter. He murmured greetings to the old man, congratulating him on looking so well, receiving in return the repeated condolences on the death of his father. As he stood, his pencil poised over his pad ready to write down the order, he had a vivid memory of his father doing the same thing, all those years ago. Taro took pride in continuing to supply the import-ant neighborhood clients in the traditional way, even though so much had changed. He took Yano-sensei's order for several kinds of sweets for a picnic-style tea meeting in the Imperial Palace grounds a week hence, asked a few questions about delivery, and bowed him out of the shop.

A couple of foreign tourists stood by the bamboo fence and gaped at this traditional Japanese transaction happening right before their eyes. Then they came in diffidently and pointed at the sign that showed photographs of the various types of shaved ice offered by the shop. Seated in the deep shade under the aw-ning, they sampled their Japanese experience with expressions that ranged from relief to awe to smugness, their conversation suitably chastened as they took in the ancient boulder and the worn wooden entranceway. One of them sketched the diamond-shaped mourning symbol on a paper napkin and put it in his pocket. Taro beamed as he peeped at them from behind the curtain. If he was attracting foreign tourists, he knew the sky was the limit. The combination of longtime local custom and the interest of foreigners would ensure the success of the sweetshop for years to come. Shintaro would inherit a flourishing business.

2005

It was a chill, cloudy day. A flurry of red leaves chased each other in front of Taro as he made his way down the street toward the shop. The season of Full Moon crackers and walnut-flavored jellied rice cakes was upon them, and the good old aromas of the shop wafted toward him.

Taro was sad and depressed. Today he had taken leave of his good friend and client Yano-sensei. The funeral had been very well-attended, neighbors from shops and classrooms all over the neighborhood, as well as Yano-sensei's considerable family and his students from years past, all crowding into the old townhouse with its formal garden. Taro was glad they had decided to hold the funeral at Yano-sensei's house in the traditional manner, instead of relegating it to one of the garish new funeral homes. Still, the solemnity of the send-off at the end, the black and gold hearse blaring its horn in melancholy farewell and the family standing motionless in black as it left, had been spoiled by a crowd of gawking foreign tourists across the narrow street. They chattered among themselves in several languages, pointing at the hearse and taking photos, as if it were a prop specially arranged for their enjoyment. This final indignity to a grand old man of the neighborhood had shaken Taro deeply.

He came in sight of the shop. He had had to remove the tiny garden because the shop next door, a newly built Western-style bakery, wanted the space for parking, but thank goodness, he had been able to keep the turtle stone. It still stood proudly between the bumpers of parked cars, showing off its bond with the centuries-old shop behind it: the Crane and Turtle Sweetshop.

At least he still had his shop and his stone to pass on to his son.

As he approached, he saw with horror that a couple of tourists, eating something on sticks, were sitting on the turtle stone. He stomped up and, waving his hands, made them understand that they were to get up and go away. They complied slowly, looking over their shoulders at the black-clad old man. A few other tourists watched the scene, and as soon as Taro went into his shop, they sat down on the boulder themselves and unwrapped their convenience store lunches.

Taro gasped with outrage. He felt dizzy and sat down at one of the little tables inside the shop. (The tables had been moved inside a few years earlier in response to loud demands from the Tourist Association for air-conditioned seating.) "Shintaro!" he called as soon as he got his breath back.

Shintaro appeared from the rear of the shop, wiping his hands on his apron. Taro scowled at the sight—kitchen aprons were not allowed in the shop during business hours, and Shintaro knew it. But he decided not to address that issue now.

"Those tourists are using the turtle stone as a chair! They are eating things on the stone out there! And not even things they bought in our shop!" he gasped. "That stone is not a park bench—it is the symbol of our shop. I've had enough. We have to do something!"

Shintaro smiled wearily. "I know, Dad, it's awful, but that stone is now on public property. It's part of the street. At least they let us keep it, that's something, isn't it?"

"Let us keep it?" The old man was beside himself. "It belongs to us! Our family and our shop have been here for generations! It's humiliating. I'm going to make a sign that says people are forbidden to sit on our turtle stone."

Shaking his head, Shintaro went back into the kitchen. He had been engaged in an experimental production of a new sweet that he hoped would bring in more custom—a cake shaped like the nearby shrine gate. He doubted if his father understood that their business was hanging by a thread. Boulder or no boulder, the place was going down.

The next day a hand-lettered sign reading, "Please do not sit on this boulder" appeared at the base of the turtle stone. Unfortunately, the sign was only in Japanese, and the foreign tourists continued to use the turtle stone as a seat as they ate their snacks and lunches.

2015

As soon as Taro awoke, he knew that it had snowed during the night. An eerie blue-white light entered his window, and utter silence pervaded the house. Taro was immediately alarmed. Where was the sound of clattering trays? Where was the scent of hot steamed wood? They ought to be preparing the New Year sweets. This was one of the busiest times of year for the Crane and Turtle Sweetshop. What laziness! These new workers were unbelievable. He threw on his clothes and stormed out of the room.

The stairs down to the shop seemed subtly different, but he negotiated them as always, moving more slowly now because of his weak legs. At the bottom, instead of a tatami room with a low table full of breakfast dishes, there was a linoleum-floored kitchen, neat as a pin, with no food in sight. Taro moved forward cautiously. This was not his home. Had he blundered into someone else's house during the night? He had better leave immediately. Shintaro and the shop staff would be waiting for him to give them their instructions for the day. There was not a moment to be lost. Everything depended on the sweets being neatly arranged and ready for customers when the shop opened.

He found an exit into the street—an unfamiliar street. At once he knew he was not dressed for this cold. He began to shiver as he limped unsteadily through the light snow, trying to see some kind of landmark. Ah! There was the shrine, the cedars still standing tall, clumps of snow sticking to their dull green sides.

And here was the corner of the shopping street. But there was no steam rising from the metal chimneys. Those lazy workers would catch it. He knew the sweetshop was three doors up on the left. His old eyes searched the side of the road for the most reliable landmark of all—the turtle stone.

It wasn't there.

Shivering with cold, Taro walked up a couple of doors more, toward the top of the street. Strangeness piled on strangeness. Instead of a dusty thoroughfare lined with wooden shops, the street was a white snowy expanse, crisscrossed with tire treads and lined with parked cars, each with its dusting of snow. Instead of shopkeepers throwing open their shutters, there was no one to be seen—the street was deserted. Was this a dream? No—if it was, he surely wouldn't be this cold—he would be still in his warm bed. He looked for something, anything familiar, but all that met his eyes was glass, concrete, and brightly colored plastic. He turned back, searching frantically now, but neither the shop nor the stone were to be seen.

Taro shouted, "Help me!" as he stumbled and fell against one of the parked cars, which immediately began an unearthly shrieking sound. His nerve gone, he started screaming, "Where is my turtle stone? Who has taken my sweetshop?" The snow and the car alarm swallowed up his cries, and he lay there, the snow melting under him, his hands prickling in the ice.

A gray-haired woman stepped out of a nearby doorway and approached him. "Oh, my goodness! Are you all right?" She crouched beside him and got a good look at his face. "It's Grand-pa Taro, isn't it? From the sweetshop? Let's get you out of this snow." She pulled at his arm and helped him struggle to his feet.

Now a young man appeared, holding out a key at arm's length. He pushed a button and the shrieking alarm stopped. He swept the snow from his car's flank, looked to see that no damage had been done, then left without a glance or word. The woman stared at him as he walked away, then took out her phone and placed a call.

"Shintaro? It's Mrs. Ueda. I found your father here in the street. He was looking for the old sweetshop. You'd better come and get him. I'll keep him in my house. He's chilled right through."

In an hour's time, Taro was sitting in a taxi, going to Shintaro's house. He still felt woozy and disoriented, but at least he wasn't cold any longer. He pulled the blanket Mrs. Ueda had lent him more tightly around his shoulders, and looked over at Shintaro.

"I don't understand . . ."

"Dad," his son replied with well-practiced patience, "I know you don't remember, but the shop had to be sold. I moved the business to Maruyoshi Department Store. And we moved you to Auntie's house. She wasn't there this morning because she had to go out. You get up and eat breakfast with her every day, and then you watch TV. You must have overslept this morning and missed her."

"What about the turtle stone?"

"Gone."

Taro hid his face in the blanket so Shintaro would not see his tears.

Shintaro looked out at the passing traffic. They would have to move Dad into a nursing home after all. He couldn't be allowed to wander around outside, he might hurt himself.

Everything was changing too fast. Shintaro felt responsibility piling up on him, squeezing his chest, making it hard to breathe. His was going to be the last generation of the shop. He himself had no children, and none of the other young people in the family wanted the burden. The grand old name of Tsuru-Kame would be no more.

He thought of the turtle stone, carted off he knew not where.

His eyes skimmed over the traffic scene outside the taxi window, then focused on a troop of tourists lugging their outsize suitcases along the sidewalk. He clenched his fists.

"Dad," he whispered, "I'm sorry."

Rhododendron Valley

The little room hummed in semidarkness. Two plastic chairs faced a bluish-white glowing screen. One was empty, the other occupied. Suzuki slouched uncomfortably and gazed at the screen, whose color reminded him of a fish belly. What kind of fish? Suzuki's head ached. He wished the doctor would come. He wanted to go home.

With a startling little rush of efficiency, the doctor—impossibly young, like a time-machine trick—breezed into the room. He perched sideways on the second chair, his whole posture that of a man who doesn't intend to stay long. Also, he was empty-handed. Wasn't he supposed to be bringing X-ray pictures to discuss? These doctors! Always changing their tune. Suzuki sighed. He wondered if he would be told to wait longer, or even to come back another day. He was used to older doctors—brisk, loud-voiced men whose hectoring manner somehow held a measure of comfort. What could such a young man possibly know?

"Suzuki-san," the doctor began, not meeting Suzuki's eyes but instead pulling a stray corner of his white coat free of his thigh and rubbing his knees with his hands. "I didn't bring the X-rays, because I think your wife should be present when we look at them. So, please go home and find out when your wife can come with you to see me, all right? Then call and make an appointment." The young doctor stood up. He was finished with Suzuki, probably already thinking about his next patient. He left the room quickly, his haste indistinguishable from relief.

"*I think your wife should be present.*" Suzuki knew only too well what this meant. The doctor was as transparent as a fish bowl; young people like him could never hide what they were thinking. Besides, it was common knowledge that doctors always called in the next of kin when the situation was hopeless. No use sugar-coating it—he was done for.

The young doctor was already out of sight when Suzuki emerged from the room. He carried his headache down the hall, out the door and into the wan spring sunlight of the hospital parking lot. The light seemed to pulse with the beat of his heart, glancing off the chrome and angles of the lined-up cars. He found his car, heaved himself into the driver's seat, and let his heavy head drop down till it rested on the steering wheel. He stayed in that position for some minutes, observing through half-closed eyes the truncated view of his lap framed by gray plastic curves, and the patches of sunlight as they brightened and faded with the passing clouds. Finally, with a sigh that seemed drawn up through the soles of his feet, he inserted the key into the slot and started the engine.

On the short drive home, his mind was like a mirror, perfectly reflecting the different-colored cars on the road, all moving independently and free of purpose. New green leaves shifted in the breeze, buildings swam up and passed by. The actions of his driving were entirely instinctive, never penetrating the mirror's surface. When he came to himself again, the car was stopped in his own driveway. Just beyond the front bumper was the rusty Roll-a-Door that now permanently covered the front of the fish shop he had run for twenty-five years. He fancied he could still smell the sharp aroma of decaying fish parts.

Slowly Suzuki got out, walked around the car, and climbed the outside steps to the flat above the shop. The flight was endless. Each rusty metal step was negotiated separately. He breathed deeply, and momentarily closed his eyes before opening the door at the top, which gave directly on the kitchen and the back view of his wife standing at the sink. She turned quickly and her eyes searched his face.

"I'm back," Suzuki said. He shuffled off his shoes and sank into a chair at the kitchen table. His feet in their socks remained motionless against the worn linoleum.

She wiped her hands on her apron and sat down opposite him. "What did they say?"

"They said I'm fine. I just need to rest a little more."

"Well, good, that's good. We can manage." She smiled at him encouragingly. Suzuki felt the mirror-self return. His wife of three decades became a blur of colors and shapes. He could not fathom her. He got up without another word and moved into the other room, where he carefully lowered himself down onto the tatami. He lay on his back, placing his head on the straw matting as gently as an egg. In a few minutes he was asleep.

Suzuki awoke in the small hours to find himself covered by a quilt. His wife slept quietly next to him. The only sounds he heard were her regular breathing and the measured tick of the clock in the kitchen. His headache had receded, and in place of the numb, dumb mirror-self of the daylight hours, his mind held a clarity so intense it was almost painful. The gloomy ceiling above him, with its old-fashioned hanging light, invited him to confess this new, secret crisis. Silently he poured out his heart. The shame of having to give up the grocery—he just didn't feel well enough to go on with it—and the greater shame of being financially dependent on his wife, which was against all his principles. And now the panicky, suffocating weight of the new situation. Her job at the supermarket was barely sufficient to keep them both from one month to the next. There was no money at all for big hospital bills, which would be useless in the end anyway.

"What should I do?" he asked the ceiling, expecting no reply.

The darkness of the night was suddenly split by a terrible, blinding thought. He gasped in shock, but then the idea came closer, vibrating with sinister attraction, and made itself his friend. This solved everything. The cost took his breath away; still, it was payable. After years of owning his own business, Suzuki was an expert in small-scale cost analysis. He communed with the ceiling all night, making his plans.

After breakfast next morning he pottered around aimlessly, still in the clothes of the previous day, waiting for his wife to go to the bus stop. In parting she urged him to take care of himself, and he answered her briefly but kindly. He watched her retreating figure obliquely from the upstairs window until she was out of sight.

He maneuvered his way downstairs and entered the storeroom at the rear of the defunct shop. Inside, it was dim and silent as an underwater cave. Half-remembered objects loomed lopsidedly at him—angles of deep freezes, stacks of discolored plastic boxes, water tanks, all wearing the same film of dust. For a moment his imagination populated the forsaken space with bustle and cheer, the chatter of the neighbors, the plump silver fish and multicolored vegetables lined up on the slanting wood shelves.

Suzuki shook himself. Whatever feelings might arise today no longer mattered. From a hook on the wall he took a coil of plastic rope, slung it over his shoulder, and grabbed up a box cutter from a shelf. He made his way through the monstrous dusty piles of junk again, emerged into the sunshine, and put the rope in the trunk of his car. Back in the tatami room upstairs, he opened the cheap freestanding closet and removed his best black suit and a shirt and tie. He folded them haphazardly into a pile. These also went into the car's trunk. Suzuki visited the flat once more, collecting his bankbook, ivory seal, and deed of ownership of the building, and putting them into a big envelope along with a few other papers. This he propped against the family altar. He was about to leave when a thought struck him. He turned back, snagged his Buddhist rosary, a circle of black stone beads, and slid it into his pocket. His actions were calm and studied. One after another, they carried him along with a precision that made him feel safe. For the first time in many days, everything was under control.

Suzuki got in his car and drove away down the street. He saw no one. The village was usually deserted on weekday mornings, and he had counted on this. He turned south toward the golf course and the mountains beyond. It was another sunny day. The mirror-self reflected gorgeous swathes of spring green, lovely little clusters of yellow dandelions by the side of the road, pools of water in the paddy fields showing the blue sky and white clouds in their depths.

He turned the car into the golf course parking lot, and backed into a space in the far corner. The lot was utterly deserted, the golf course having closed the previous year. Suzuki placed a shade over the windshield and sat in the dim interior of the car. The windows were open and the delicious spring breeze wafted in and out. Now that he was here, he found he couldn't bear to carry out his plan in daylight. He would have to wait until nightfall. He sat motionless during the hours it took the sun to pass across the sky. Finally evening shadows began to gather around him. As the last bars of sunlight disappeared from the parking lot, Suzuki slowly stirred, removed the window shade, and tossed it into the back seat. He started the engine and drove out of the parking lot.

A little further up the mountain road, a small sign reading "Rhododendron Valley" indicated a road off to the left. Suzuki drove quietly along under the trees, negotiating the curves, gliding through the deepening twilight like a fish through dark water. Reaching a wide spot in the road, he pulled in, parked, and got out. The breeze had vanished with the sun, and everything was utterly still. The air was cool and the little mauve-colored clouds overhead seemed very far away. Suzuki opened the trunk, and slowly changed into his best clothes, transferring the rosary to his suit coat pocket. As he knotted his tie, his face craned upward, and he felt the unbearable sweetness and glory of his flesh. His eyes swam with tears.

Suzuki struggled to regain the blessedly unfeeling mirror-self that had brought him this far. Finally he succeeded. Taking up the coil of rope, he turned in the dusk and began trudging up a footpath that bordered a small stream. Rain had been keeping off in recent weeks, and the stream was just a chain of shallow pools, motionless, faintly glowing. The rhododendrons on the other side of the stream were a bank of shadow, their blooms still a few weeks away. Suzuki climbed steadily. It took him about ten minutes to reach the end of the little path, which petered out for no particular reason next to a bench and a signpost.

His good shoes slipping on the carpet of leaves, Suzuki angled upward, away from the path, and hauled himself up the slope by gripping the trunks of small trees. He cast around for a few minutes, and soon found what he was looking for. Calmly he measured the rope, cut it with the box cutter, and tied one end to a large stone at the base of a suitably forked tree. The other end he tied around his neck, above the collar, and settled the knot snugly under his ear. Then he bent down and rigged a small platform of rocks and fallen branches to stand on. Huffing a little, he climbed onto these, hefting the rope-tied stone in his arms. Then he carefully wedged the stone into the fork of the tree, working by touch since it was now almost full dark.

Suzuki stood unmoving on the pile of stones, fingering the beads in his pocket. He looked up, and the silky air and far high stars made him feel transparent. He had done his work, his preparations were complete. All the hours, minutes, and seconds of his life came down to this. There remained only the deed itself. He took one deep breath, then with a heave, he pushed the big stone through the fork of the tree, at the same time kicking aside the makeshift platform under his feet. Light exploded behind his eyes as the rope tightened. Last of all he felt the tree bark graze his cheek. His feet in their good shoes jangled crazily for a moment, then were still. The trees all around looked down on him, and silence returned to the woods as he joined the night.

Uncle Trash

LOCAL MAN GETS ATTENTION

Yomitori News, May 20

A resident of Setagaya Ward has been the focus of neighborhood attention recently. Mr. Kenzo Nishimura, age 75, has earned the local nickname "Uncle Trash" because of his longtime hoarding activities.

Mr. Nishimura has been hoarding various objects for decades, but his stash has recently become so voluminous that it is noticeable to passersby. A neighbor, who prefers that we not use her name, is the source of our story. She knocked on Mr. Nishimura's door to collect fees for NHK Television, and saw head-high piles of old newspapers crowding the entranceway of his home. When interviewed by our reporter, the neighbor said Mr. Nishimura was barely able to squeeze between the piles to come out and talk to her.

Stacks of buckets and boxes have also recently begun appearing in the small front yard. Children coming home from school have begun to stop in front of Mr. Nishimura's house and call out "Uncle Trash! Why do you have so much trash in your house?" Neighbors heard the nickname, and it is now in common use throughout the area.

A reporter from this newspaper visited the house to interview him. Mr. Nishimura, who lives alone but has a daughter and son-in-law living in the neighborhood, said that he has collected a whole houseful of items that other people would consider "trash," including 36 plastic buckets, 110 pairs of old shoes, several cabinets full of shopping bags, and old newspapers and magazines dating back to the early 1970s.

"I don't think of it as trash myself, though," he remarked. "To me these objects are like my children. I take care of them, organize them, and never abandon any of them."

Asked how he felt about the nickname, Mr. Nishimura said "I don't mind."

The daughter and son-in-law of "Uncle Trash" declined to be interviewed.

The head of the block association, Mr. Fumio Takahashi, said that at present, everyone is okay with Mr. Nishimura's strange hobby, but that he will have to stop if it is determined that the house has become a neighborhood fire hazard.

By our Staff Reporter

"UNCLE TRASH" HOME TO APPEAR ON TELEVISION

Yomitori News, June 17

Mr. Kenzo Nishimura, known locally as "Uncle Trash," will have his home featured in an episode of the popular show *Hoarders Banzai* on Yomitori Television at the end of this month.

The show picks out the home of a well-known hoarder and a cleanup crew goes into the house, getting rid of all the trash, and doing any necessary repairs. The shows always end with the hoarder in tears, thanking the show's host and saying they never could have done it on their own.

This newspaper has discovered that Mr. Nishimura's home was put up for the show by his son-in-law, Mr Yuji Kanemoto, who lives nearby. After reading our previous article (May 20), Mr. Kanemoto agreed to speak to our reporter about the decision to put the house on TV.

"We are concerned about Grandpa," he said. "He can barely turn around in that house, there is so much trash." He indicated that another reason he contacted the TV show was that the station pays "thank-you money" to the person who submitted a house for consideration. "We are going to get two hundred thousand yen for this," said Mr. Kanemoto. "We will use it for Grandpa's medical bills." He did admit that so far, Mr. Nishimura has had no major medical problems. "It's for the future," he explained.

The cleanup will be filmed on June 27 and will be televised at 7:30 pm on July 10, on Yomitori Television.

By our Staff Reporter

TV FILMING OF HOARDER'S HOME IN SETAGAYA
Yomitori News, June 28

The home of the well-known Setagaya hoarder, "Uncle Trash," was cleaned out today by the film crew of the popular TV program *Hoarders Banzai*. The entire neighborhood turned out to watch the cleaning and filming (*see photos, page 12*).

Mr. Kenzo Nishimura, the famous "Uncle Trash," was conspicuous by his absence. His son-in-law, Mr. Yuji Kanemoto, said he had treated him to a weekend at a hot spring resort. Mr. Nishimura is expected to return to his home on the first of next month.

Twelve dumpsters had been filled to the brim by the time the cleanup, which lasted all day, was finished. Cleanup crew members were quoted as saying they were grateful that "Uncle Trash" didn't have any organic waste in his hoarded trash, so there was little unpleasant smell. The vast majority of the trash was old paper. Next most numerous were old clothes, followed by plastic items of various types. Mr. Kanemoto, Mr. Nishimura's son-in-law, who remained on the scene from start to finish, said he was unaware of any valuables kept in the home.

After the cleanup, the TV crew moved some new furniture into the house, including a flat-screen TV and a sofa and chairs. A brand new bed has replaced Mr. Nishimura's old futons. This is a service provided by the TV show, in addition to the two hundred thousand yen "thank you money" given to Mr. Kanemoto as the applicant.

"Grandpa will be very surprised and pleased by the result of the cleanup," said Mr. Kanemoto. "It looks like a completely different house."

The TV crew will return to the house on July 1 to film Mr. Nishimura's reaction to the cleanup.

By our Staff Reporter

MAN HOSPITALIZED AFTER NEIGHBORHOOD FRACAS

Yomitori News, July 2

In Setagaya Ward yesterday, an elderly man was hospitalized after he went berserk and tried to assault several people.

Mr. Kenzo Nishimura, the popular local "Uncle Trash" figure, returned to his home yesterday after several days' vacation in the Karuizawa hot spring resort. During his absence, his son-in-law, Mr. Yuji Kanemoto, supervised the televised cleanup of Mr. Nishimura's home, which had become silted up with decades' worth of trash. He said he had intended it as a surprise for his father-in-law.

The TV crew returned yesterday to film Mr. Nishimura's reaction to his newly cleaned house, which had also been spiffed up with several new pieces of furniture, courtesy of the TV station.

Unfortunately, when Mr. Nishimura entered his house and saw the changes, he became confused and violent, screaming "My children! You have taken away my children! Where are they?" and punching everyone within reach. The assistant producer of the show, Mr. Seiji Ito, received a black eye, and the film crew barely managed to save their video camera from breakage. After some minutes, Mr. Nishimura, who was bleeding from the nose, was subdued by an ambulance crew and driven to a nearby hospital.

Interviewed by this reporter, Mr. Ito said, "We certainly didn't expect this kind of reaction. Most people who appear on our show are very happy to have their houses cleaned. We have decided not to air the film of Mr. Nishimura's negative reaction to the cleanup. Instead, we will feature Mr. Kanemoto, who gave us a final interview thanking us for our help in cleaning and arranging his father's home." The follow-up TV show will be aired on July 10.

By our Staff Reporter

"UNCLE TRASH" IS AT IT AGAIN

Yomitori News, December 12

Readers will recall the story of "Uncle Trash" of Setagaya Ward, whose house was featured in the TV series *Hoarders Banzai* in July of this year. After the house was cleaned in his absence, Mr. Kenzo Nishimura returned from a vacation to find his house transformed. He thereupon became agitated and had to be hospitalized, finally returning to the house on July 5.

Since then, Mr. Nishimura has redoubled his efforts to collect trash and store it in his home. He has even been observed by neighbors carting off stacks of old newspapers left for the recycler.

Mr. Nishimura declined to comment when approached by our reporter, so his son-in-law, Mr. Yuji Kanemoto, was interviewed instead. Mr. Kanemoto appeared disappointed that the hoarding has continued and even escalated after the televised cleanup in the summer. "I really thought Dad would turn over a new leaf," he said. "But at this rate, I wouldn't be surprised if the house is full again by the end of the year." Mr. Kanemoto further intimated that because his father-in-law was becoming senile, and might pose a danger to himself and others, he would be moved into his son-in-law's house early in the New Year. The present house, he said, would be sold. Mr. Kanemoto expects to get a good price for the house, as it has achieved a certain fame due to being the focus of a TV program.

When last seen, Mr. Nishimura was dragging a fresh load of

old newspapers into his house by the front door. He declined to be interviewed, and shut the door in the cameraman's face.

By our Staff Reporter

MYSTERIOUS MIDNIGHT BLAZE AND DEATH OF SETAGAYA RESIDENT

Yomitori News, December 27

In Setagaya Ward last night, firefighters responding to a call at 11:57 pm arrived to find a blaze in the entranceway of the house of well-known hoarder Mr. Kenzo Nishimura, otherwise known as "Uncle Trash." The fire was extinguished within minutes.

However, once the fire was out, the body of Mr. Yuji Kanemoto, the resident's son-in-law, was discovered lying face down in the entranceway, buried under a huge mound of old newspapers. He appeared to have been overcome by fumes, as his body was not burned at all.

Police say the investigation is likely to bring a result of "death by misadventure." They postulate that Mr. Kanemoto was entering the house to check on Mr. Nishimura, made a wrong step, and brought the high stacks of old newspapers down on himself. They are still investigating the cause of the fire.

Mr. Nishimura was seen carrying old newspapers into his house at sunset yesterday, but now he seems to have disappeared. If anyone in the neighborhood has any information, the police ask that they contact the station immediately.

By our Staff Reporter

Watch Again

Osaka Station is full of noise, right up to its big domed roof. Roar of trains coming and going, screech of brakes, scurrying feet of commuters, jumbled PA voices. Halfway down the platform, Yuko is waiting to board the train that will take her home. She's a tall, slim, fresh-faced girl in her late twenties, wearing white, her hair tied back with a couple of loose strands moving gently in the breeze created by all this commotion.

The train arrives and the doors slide open with a hiss. Standing room only, as usual. Yuko is glad that tonight she got off early from her job, and will have a peaceful evening without rushing through her dinner and bath. She can feel her body relaxing into the pleasantly unstructured time ahead. She stands easily in the aisle of the train, midway between the doors, holding one of the plastic handles affixed to the seat backs.

She scans the occupied seats around her, determining with a practiced eye if any of the nearby seated passengers are making preparations to get off at the next station. Suddenly, her ears roar with shock as she sees a familiar head in the window seat in the next row up. It's actually only the back of the head she sees, but that's enough. She's married to it, after all. That's Hiroshi, her estranged husband. She hasn't seen him in a month.

All Yuko's defenses go up. She spins a cloak of silence around her, stepping back into the role of the anonymous commuter that she assumes twice a day. She wills herself to think like a commuter, planning her solitary dinner and considering the lineup of

TV shows on offer that evening.

But what's he doing? It looks as if he has pushed his mobile phone into the backrest cover of the seat in front, and is watching some kind of video. Tiny white cords snake from the phone to his ears. He's got his arms crossed, slouching in the seat.

In spite of herself, Yuko is curious. Holding her breath, she moves a tiny bit forward, and focuses on the screen of the mobile phone, partially obscured by the white stretchy material of the seat cover. The video finishes and "Watch again" flashes on the screen. Hiroshi leans forward and touches it, then settles back again. Yuko strains to see.

It's an indoor scene, an amateur cameraman shooting between large, out-of-focus shoulders. Three people stand together in the middle distance, their clothes black on the right, white on the left . . . It's a wedding. The figure in the middle, a portly man, raises his hand and the couple, now resolved into the bride and groom, lean toward each other in a kiss. There's a flurry on the screen as people around the cameraman begin to applaud. The newly married couple turn to face their audience, and raise their joined hands like people who have won a race, their faces radiant.

It's Yuko and Hiroshi. It's the video of their wedding, taken by Hiroshi's friend Daiki.

The video ends, the "Watch Again" logo flashes on the screen, and again Hiroshi leans forward. Yuko watches as he plays the video over and over. The little clip, barely two minutes long, keeps repeating. Then Yuko notices something else. Hiroshi's hands have crept up to his face as he watches, and are pressed against his cheeks. Could he be crying? Suddenly she comes to with a start, realizing that her station is approaching.

She goes to the door behind her so she won't pass Hiroshi on her way out, and leaves in a rush. Her mind is in a whirl, remembering, recalling.

"Hi. This class is really interesting, isn't it?"

"I like it."

"And the teacher is so entertaining. You never know what she's going to say next."

"Yes. Say, I've seen you in some other classes. Are you a first-year student?"

"Sociology. My name's Yuko, by the way."

"I'm Hiroshi. So, where are you from, Yuko?"

"Oh, I'm a city girl. From Moriguchi in Osaka. How about you?"

"Oh, you probably commute to school. I don't, I have an apartment. I'm from all the way up in Tohoku—Aomori."

"Heavens! That's where the apples come from, isn't it?"

"Well, yes, although my parents are rice farmers."

"Here comes the teacher. Want to get lunch today?"

"Um—all right."

"Wait for me after class. I'll see you at the front door."

"Hello, Yuko."

"Hi, Hiroshi. Thanks for last night. I had a really good time."

"Well, I thought we ought to mark our anniversary. A month since the day we met!"

"Time flies when you're having fun! Anyway, the movie was great. Really made me think. I enjoyed our discussion afterwards, too."

"It's nice to talk to someone from the heart. I haven't had that experience much."

"I think communication is so important between friends."

"And that's just what we are. Coming to class?"

"Hi, Hiroshi. How are the finals going?"

"Well, I think I did okay on the English exam. How about you?"

"I did all right, but I know my reports won't be ready on time! So much work . . . I'm so tired. Do you mind if we just stay in tonight?"

"Your place or mine?"

"Mine—okay? We'll order in some sushi or something."

"I'm so glad you moved into your own apartment. It's nice to have a choice of places. Are you feeling all right now?"

"Yes, I just don't feel like going out anywhere."

"You know . . . what would be really nice . . . "

"What?"

"Being together all the time."

"I have to say, I've been thinking the same thing."

"I feel so easy with you . . . I can say anything, do anything. I think I want that all my life."

"Well, it's only a few months till graduation. When we find jobs, we can think about getting married."

"You're so practical. I love that about you. Come here."

"Hiroshi! Wait until we get home. People are watching!"

Yuko climbs the steps of the station and passes through the wicket to the street. They were so happy at first! The only shadow on their budding relationship had been cast by meeting his parents. That long, long train trip with Hiroshi, the dark cavernous old-fashioned house, the bugs, oh my god, the bugs! His father, a blunt, close-mouthed old man, never saying a word unless he was barking out orders. "Get me some beer! This beer's not cold! Get me some tea! Get the bath ready!" His mother, scurrying around with an unreadable face, doing her husband's bidding. A house with no humor and definitely no heartfelt communication. No wonder Hiroshi had been so hungry for it.

And the wedding. All their friends from university and their jobs were there, her colleagues from the clothing outlet, his from the electronics company. Beautiful wedding hall, everything just as they wanted it—and in the middle, crouching like a couple of spiders, his parents. Dressed in their decades-old finery, glaring about them at all the newness and what they obviously judged to be profligate spending, without a word to anyone except during the formal toasts. Even the presence of Hiroshi's brother and a few relatives did nothing to diminish their fish-out-of-water awkwardness. Yuko's parents had been dumbfounded. They liked Hiroshi and were glad their daughter had found someone she loved to be married to. They couldn't understand why his parents did nothing but scowl. It was the country way, Hiroshi whispered to his bride, not to show feelings of happiness lest the people around you feel insulted or jealous. Hard work and endurance had always been the order of the day for them. The two sets of parents would never be able to understand each other.

The first year of the marriage was mostly fine. Hiroshi sometimes talked in a disappointed way about how Yuko didn't get pregnant. She herself didn't want a child right away, she wanted to continue with her absorbing work a little longer before starting a family, but it seemed he was a bit old-fashioned in his thinking. This was one thing they had never really discussed, although they had talked about every other subject under the sun during their courtship and engagement.

Then the time of uneasiness and silence began. She winces as she recalls how uncomfortable their relationship suddenly became.

"I'm home."

"Hi, Hiroshi. We've got roast chicken tonight!"

". . ."

"Your favorite. How was your day?"

"Nothing special . . ."

"I've had such a tiring day . . . my boss asked so many questions! Here you go. Do you want a beer with your dinner?"

"This chicken came from the shop across the street, didn't it?"

"*Well, yes. I just got home myself a half hour ago. I didn't have time to cook.*"

"*No time to cook . . .*"

"*I'm home.*"

"*Hi, Hiroshi. How was your day?*"

"*What's for dinner?*"

"*Sushi.*"

"*. . .*"

"*How was your day?*"

"*Lots of problems. I don't want to talk about it.*"

"*Here you go. Want a beer? I'm having one.*"

"*What? You didn't cook again? No cooking, no babies . . . what kind of wife are you?*"

"*Oh, Hiroshi. How can you say that? You know I work as hard as you do.*"

"*. . .*"

"*I'm home. Sorry I'm late.*"

"*. . .*"

"*Hiroshi? I'm sorry I'm late. We had a meeting at work and it went on so long . . .*"

"*. . .*"

"*Here's some croquettes from the butcher. You know you like them.*"

"*Where have you been?*"

"*I told you. We had a meeting. If it comes to that, why are you home so early?*"

"*. . .*"

"*Well? This is the first time you've been home before nine this month.*"

"*Don't ask me. I don't want to talk about it.*"

"*Well, here's your dinner. We can have that salad from yesterday with it.*"

"*. . .*"

"Do you want a beer? Hiroshi? Hey! What are you doing! Look at this mess! Our dinner, all over the floor!"

"You never cook for me! Why don't you ever cook for me?"

"Stop it! What's gotten into you?"

" . . ."

"Okay. I'm not staying here if that's how you're going to be. I'm going to my sister's. Get your own dinner."

"Yuko! Telephone for you!"

"Hello?"

"Yuko? It's Hiroshi."

"What makes you think I want to talk to you?"

"Please, just hear me out."

"What's the matter with you these days?"

"I don't know. Troubles at work."

"Well, why don't you tell me? Why don't you talk to me? You used to talk to me."

"I don't know . . . please come home. I'm sorry. I'll try to do better."

"Well . . . OK. I'll be home after work tonight. And Hiroshi?"

"What?"

"I can't go on with you if you're going to yell and throw things around. You understand that, don't you? And if you have problems, you have to tell me about them. That's the kind of marriage I want."

"OK. See you tonight."

"I'm home. Hiroshi! Why are you back so early?"

" . . ."

"Oh no. Not this again. I have some good news tonight and I want you to listen."

"What is it?"

"I finally got promoted! My boss says I'm doing great work and I'm going to be at the head office starting next month!"

" . . ."

"Don't you have anything to say?"

"I guess you'll be home less than ever now."

"What do you mean?"

"No dinner, no children, you hardly even have time to clean. Look at this place!"

"But both of us are working hard at jobs we like. We don't have much time to ourselves, but that's natural at the beginning. We'll have time later on—"

"Huh! Do you want to know what MY day was like? Because I have some news too."

"What is it?"

"I almost lost my job! I got a warning from the boss!"

"Oh, Hiroshi. How awful for you."

"He said I was too short-tempered with the staff. Of course I'm short-tempered! I work so much, I hardly have time to breathe, and then when I do get home . . ."

"What? When you do get home, what?"

"My wife isn't there! Or if she is, she just feeds me on crap! Never does anything I say! Always prancing around bragging about her wonderful job!"

"You can't be serious!"

"I'll show you how serious I am!"

"Hiroshi! What are you doing! Stop it! Stop breaking things!"

" . . ."

"If you don't stop . . ."

" . . ."

"Oh! Look what you did! Smashed my very favorite coffee mug! Don't you remember buying this for me? Okay, that's all. Let me out. Get out of my way!"

Yuko turns the key in the lock of her apartment door. For a month she has been happy on her own, self-contained, and busy at her work. She often wonders about Hiroshi, because she genuinely loves him. But when he stopped talking to her, when he started to say mean things and break her treasured objects, she had no choice but to leave. Still, she misses him as he used to be, misses their companionship. What caused him to change so drastically?

She lets herself in and turns on the lights. She puts down her things and, going into the little kitchen, puts some water in the electric kettle for a cup of coffee. As usual, she feels a twinge of pain at the thought that her favorite red coffee mug is no more. While waiting for the water to boil, she moves around the kitchen, washing her hands and tidying up. She makes a cup of tea in her second-favorite mug and carries it into the living room, thinking to turn on the TV to catch the news.

That's when she sees it. A face looking in from the balcony. Low down, as though the person is sitting on the concrete just outside the glass sliding door.

With a frisson of horror, Yuko moves toward her bag and her phone. *I have to call the police.*

But wait. Could that be . . . Hiroshi? It is. She sinks down onto the sofa, her legs weak with reaction and relief. She looks at his face—it's tear-stained. *So he was crying in the train,* she thinks. *But how did he get here? How did he know where I was?*

These thoughts are a little disturbing, but it is her husband, the man she loves, on the other side of the glass. She approaches the sliding door, unlocks it, and opens it a crack. There is still a locked screen door between them. She sits down on the floor inside the door, just a few inches from him. "What are you doing here?"

"Please don't be angry. I saw you getting off the train, and I followed you."

"I saw you in the train."

"Why didn't you say something? I would have, if I'd seen you."

"I don't know. I guess I'm still angry with you. You behaved so badly the last few months we were together. Maybe I was a little scared too."

He looks down. "I've missed you so much, Yuko."

"Well, I haven't missed you. Not the way you were then."

A couple of minutes of silence falls, and she can hear him sniffling. *People say women are weak, but it's men who are weak. We're the strong ones really.* "Hiroshi. What changed? How come everything was so good for a while and then it all went so wrong? I don't think I changed—but you did. Why?"

He gulps, and she senses that he is getting up his courage. Finally he murmurs, "I got a letter from my dad. He was asking when the grandchildren would be coming along. He said a woman who didn't have children was worth nothing. He said all kinds of awful things about you."

"Oh, Hiroshi."

"I hated him—but I hated you too. I thought in many ways he was right. *My* mother never took an outside job. She waited on us hand and foot, cooked every day, raised us kids, was always there. I got to thinking how different our married life was—yours and mine."

His voice is hesitant, and she knows he is speaking from the heart. She lets out a deep breath. She hasn't heard this candid, sweet voice of his for months. In reply, she chooses her words carefully.

"I see . . . and, so, Hiroshi, do you think your parents are happy? Do you think your mother is happy? Has she had a good life?"

He doesn't reply.

"Do you think your parents have a better marriage than we do?"

Still no reply, but she can hear him crying.

"When we were students together, you always said how happy you were to be able to speak your mind and communicate freely at last. I guess you didn't have much of that when you were living at home."

He nods, and wipes his eyes with his sleeve.

She feels her own eyes filling with tears. "So what we had was better. It was. Say it."

"What we had was better."

She lets out another long breath. He continues, spilling out the words.

"It was my job, too. Suddenly it all seemed overwhelming. After student life, it was so different. Pressure, responsibilities. I couldn't handle it."

"Well, but you never told me you were having trouble. I could have helped you."

"I guess so. But you know, my dad, he never talked, never complained . . ."

"As far as you know. You didn't see their whole relation-ship, only what a child sees. Hiroshi, we have to grow up now. We have to figure out how our lives will be. We can't take our parents as our models. We have to do it ourselves. Decide what we want."

"Well . . . do you want kids?"

"Eventually, of course! But I just want a little time to myself, you know, to have my job and see if I could be a success at it."

"How's it going these days?"

"It's fine. But I've had to get used to late nights, I'm usually not home so early."

"Me neither," he responds with a little sound that is like a laugh. "I happened to have the day off today because there was a funeral for one of the supervisors."

"So that's why you were riding the train and watching our wedding video over and over?"

"You saw that? Yuko . . . I've made such a mess of things. What can I do to fix them? Oh—one thing I can do. Here." He pulls a small package wrapped in brown paper from a satchel beside him, and places it on the door frame. "Will you take it?"

She looks at the irregular package, which is quite crushed. It must have been in the bag for a long time. She thinks very hard for a moment.

"Hiroshi, I can't open this door. You know that."

He looks ashamed.

"But I'd like to see you again. We need to talk. Can you come to the Star Café on Sunday? The one near our old apartment?"

"Sunday? That's our second wedding anniversary."

"Yes, it is. I'll meet you there. Say eleven o'clock."

He gets up and puts the satchel over his shoulder. "I'll go now."

She gets up too, so they are standing face to face, looking at each other through the glass. "How did you get up to the balcony, anyway?"

"Oh, I climbed up. It isn't really that hard." They both giggle a little. Then he goes to the balcony and cautiously eases himself over the edge, and disappears.

Yuko waits for the sounds of his departure to die away. Then she unlocks the screen and picks up the little package. She locks both doors again—*is it really so easy to climb onto the balcony? That's unsettling*—and unwraps the package as she walks toward the kitchen.

In her hand is a red coffee mug, the twin of the one that was broken.

Showa Girl

A sharp bird call scattered Misako's dream. A moment later, her eyes popped open in response to the pressure of daylight. She knew she couldn't stay in her snug futon any longer. The futon next to hers was empty, and the muted sound of Mother preparing breakfast came to her ears, as the rich salty scent of miso soup drifted to her nose.

Mother's voice, faint through two sets of paper doors, called her to get up. She was expected to help in the kitchen. Misako threw the quilt back and, shivering, stepped out of her night kimono and folded it sketchily, placing it on her little bran-filled pillow. At the same moment she remembered her dream—something about a fight with the next-door children—and shook her head vigorously to dispel it, her straight black hair flying around her face like a little fan. Quickly she found her clothes and pulled them on, then slid open the door and ran barefoot into the outer room. With a brief "good morning" to Mother standing at the

stove, Misako stepped down to the earthen floor of the kitchen, maneuvered her feet into wooden clogs, and went out into the sunshine to wash her face. The basin of water stood on the wellhead as usual, big puffy clouds reflected in its surface. As she reached blindly for the hanging towel, face dripping, gasping with cold, she could smell plum blossom. It was March, and today was the last day of the school year.

Father came clumping into the yard. He was big and rugged, with a calm, ugly face. He had been preparing for the rice planting, still a month away. He swept his daughter up and carried her back into the kitchen. She giggled, looking straight down into the soup pot from the impossible height of his warm homespun shoulder. When she had slithered down to the floor again, Mother frowned at her absently through a cloud of steam. "Go and wake up Teacher, he can't be late for school, today of all days."

Misako shuffled out of her clogs, climbed up to the living area floor, and knelt and reached down, carefully lining up the clogs before scampering off down the corridor. She might be only six years old, but she knew what her mother meant. No one could be late on the last day, especially a teacher. She felt a child's precarious self-importance: the schoolteacher lived right in her house! She slid the door open a crack and peeped in with bright eyes. "Time to get up!" she cried. The mound of quilt on the floor twitched suddenly, almost as if her voice had come into his dream like the song of a bird. The thought made her giggle, and then his tousled head appeared and she tiptoed rapidly away, half exhilarated and half afraid.

A few minutes later, as she helped her mother set the table, Teacher came in and, as usual, bowed slightly and greeted the parents formally before settling in his place, crossing his legs with rough adolescent movements. He was a very young teacher, and Misako thought him unbearably handsome, with his level brow and beautifully shaped lips. Her mother was filling bowls with a wooden paddle from the steaming iron pot, mounding the rice and fluffing it up just so, and Misako passed the bowls around the table. When all were served with soup and rice, they paused for a word of thanks before beginning the meal. Father talked to Teacher, and although Misako tried to listen, she was distracted by her mother's muted directions—pass your father the pickles; get Teacher's bowl, he wants a refill—and in any case, she could hardly understand a word of the talk. One word, though, kept recurring: "Manchuria." She wondered what it meant.

Teacher finished his breakfast with a word of thanks, and returned to his room, emerging a moment later wearing his jacket and carrying his book bag. Misako glanced at him as she carried dirty dishes carefully into the kitchen. She wished she were old enough to go to school, so she could be in his class and see him more than just a few minutes each morning and evening. He stepped into his shoes and opened the front door, murmuring the customary words.

"I'm going, and I'll come back."

The mother raised her eyes from the washing bucket to answer him, "Please go and come back." Then, as the door closed, she admonished Misako, "Go and get the rest of the dishes! I want you to finish this job. I have to change my clothes."

Misako took over her mother's task, finally struggling out the door with the wash water, which she dumped on the stone flags outside. She paused, stretching her back in unconscious imitation of Mother, who would be busy in the vegetable patch this morning, clearing out the rest of the cabbages and starting the work of preparing the land for the summer vegetables. Misako would be helping, carrying the cabbages, fetching the tools her mother wanted. She looked up at the spring sky with its white clouds like saturated sponges. Her dream came back to her, and she wondered again why the children next door were always bullying and teasing her, calling her "Princess" and other sarcastic names until she cried.

Her mother's voice cut through her musings, and she ran out to the vegetable patch in front of the house.

Misako flung the lightweight quilt off. The summer sun, already high in the sky, illuminated the plump, fine-skinned fourteen-year-old as she hurried to dress. The school term was ending, and she had a record of perfect attendance which was her pride and joy. But she had a lot to do before she could hop on her bicycle and pedal off to the middle school.

Stepping into wooden clogs in the kitchen, she went out into the sunshine to wash her face and draw another basin of water for the next person. No time now to look up at the clouds or listen for birdsong. Back inside, she put water on the stove to heat for soup, fetched pickles from the pickle bed in its brown ceramic pot, and set the rice mixed with millet, soaked overnight, on another stove burner to cook, all with smooth, practiced movements.

She set the table for two. As always, this gave her a pang. Father had passed away just a few months earlier, and she missed his rugged love. Also, Teacher was not there. Before her eighth birthday, he had disappeared from the house. Her father had told her that Teacher had gone to Manchuria to help set up a school in the new Japanese colony. Then the war had come, and since then, no one had heard a thing. Misako heard people say he must be dead. She and her mother went on with the housework together. Their experience was not unusual—every house in the village was short of able-bodied men. The rapid changes of the years had dazed them all.

She clearly remembered the mustering of the local boys as they boarded buses to be taken to the train station and then off to war. And their mothers, dressed in their best with blinding white aprons, waving little Rising Sun flags distributed by the government, the fluttering red and white hiding the faces fighting back tears. The buses departed, and the women dispersed to their homes, closing the doors so they could be alone with their grief and anxiety. The radios blasted out martial music and barked reports of victory. Sometimes the air was full of the drone of small airplanes taking off from the airstrip in the next town.

And then, sudden silence.

The kind of silence that follows an enormous noise.

Misako didn't live close enough to hear the two giant detonations that ended the war, but she heard the silence. People discussed Japan's surrender in muted tones. There were muttered lamentations about the awful waste of lives and resources, and muttered speculation—what would happen to them now? She herself hoped that the postwar era would include more food. They had more food here in the countryside than people in the towns did, but still, delicious treats hardly ever came her way.

Breakfast over, Misako gathered her school books, pencil and notebook, and rushed out the door with a hurried "I'm going, I'll be back." Her mother, slower now, answered in the usual way as she washed the breakfast dishes.

As she cycled through the cool morning, Misako reflected that one at least of her childhood mysteries had been solved. Two years before, upon entering middle school, the office lady had gone over some official papers with her. She had peeked at them and discovered, beside her name, the word "Adopted." That day, her anxiety had nothing to do with the hunger and sadness which increased with each passing month of war. She went to her mother for an explanation. Tearfully, the mother revealed what she had hidden from her daughter for so many years. Misako had been born in the house next door, the youngest of five children. At the time of her birth, her biological mother had been ill, and had asked her sister, married, childless, and living next door, to care for the child. By the time the illness had passed, the sister was so attached to little Misako that an adoption was arranged. Misako's adoptive mother and father were happy to have her, even if she was a girl; they could always find someone's younger son to marry her and take on the house and family name. That was the pattern, as Misako had heard time and again. The eldest son inherited the house, while the younger sons went off to find some other house to inherit by marrying the eldest girl from a family with daughters. Their own family had been without sons for almost a century; her adoptive father had married into the family as well. Child trading and marital machinations among the relatives' houses in the village had gone on constantly as long as anyone could remember. The houses were the important thing, the continuity of inheritance.

No wonder the kids next door had always been so mean to her. She had been singled out to be just one child in a family, no fighting over supper, no hand-me-downs, no sharing, doted on as only an only child can be. Of course they must have been jealous.

And who would she herself marry? She shrugged at the pointless question. It wasn't up to her.

The rice fields began to give way to buildings speeding past on either side. School was not far away now. She stopped at an intersection to let a few motorcycles pass, not thinking about anything in particular, her mind full of the school day ahead. The street was clear and she stepped up on her bike pedals, ready to ride on. It was then that it happened.

Two big, muscled American soldiers from the local base (actually just a house with half a dozen soldiers living in it—a very small rural outpost of the Occupation Forces) moved toward her, white teeth flashing. One of them grabbed her bike handlebars, preventing her from going forward. The other was laughing and talking in a loud voice. Misako didn't understand a word. She stood, head lowered, heart thumping, waiting until the teasing was over and they stepped back. Her vision blurred as she rode away.

Two years later, Misako was about to graduate from middle school. One day, returning home, she barely had time to hop off her bicycle before her mother appeared, breathless, and grasped her arm.

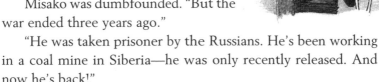

"You'll never guess who was here today!" Her mother gazed at her with excited eyes, then without waiting for an answer, she blurted, "Teacher! He's back from the war!"

Misako was dumbfounded. "But the war ended three years ago."

"He was taken prisoner by the Russians. He's been working in a coal mine in Siberia—he was only recently released. And now he's back!"

"We all thought he was dead. Didn't we?"

"We did. But he's alive! He came this afternoon to say hello. He was devastated to hear that Father was gone. He went over to next door as well." The mother paused significantly, and Misako understood her right away. As a young teacher, he had made no secret of his interest in the second-eldest girl next door, Hanako, barely a teenager at the time. It was obvious he had come back to inquire about her.

A few days later, Misako and her mother learned that Teacher had indeed asked for Hanako's hand. Hanako had been so embarrassed that she ran upstairs and hid. The reason was that she was already married. Just after the war ended, she had been married to a cousin, and she already had a baby. Teacher had left, disappointed.

Some days later, a letter arrived for Mother, addressed in handwriting that Misako recognized as Teacher's. Mother took it next door to discuss with the other family members. The letter contained a proposal of marriage to Misako. "No—he's too old for her" was the verdict, and Teacher was notified of the decision by letter.

Misako herself saw the next letter. Teacher pleaded to be allowed to join the family. Misako knew instinctively that this was no love-struck young man pining for his beloved. He was a hardheaded thirtysomething now, with a lot of painful experience behind him, wanting only to settle down in a peaceful place with good memories and take up the threads of his life.

Misako's mother was weak, tired and ill. She longed for a man in the house again, and this time she agreed to the marriage. Thus Teacher and the little girl who had woken him up at the age of six were married. She was sixteen and he was thirty-two, exactly twice her age.

Author's note: This is the end of Showa Girl's story, as upon her marriage she became Showa Woman. She eventually had four children, including two boys, the first male children to be born in the family in a century. Though her marriage was not as happy as she had hoped (her husband brought back a violent temper from his years in prison), she had a long, full life, with a few adventures, and even some overseas trips. Perhaps she would have said that her greatest adventure was that her beloved elder son, who inherited the house, brought home a true foreigner, a girl from Australia, to be his bride.

Showa Girl was my mother-in-law.

A Year of
Coffee and Cake

1

Amanda paused with a double-fisted bouquet of silverware, halfway from the cardboard box to the drawer. She peeped through the as-yet-uncurtained kitchen window. The house next door appeared to be a mirror image of her own, its bland façade giving nothing away. Someone was shouting continuously somewhere in the back—someone who sounded very old and very angry.

The shouts were in Japanese, of course. After ten years in the country, Amanda could understand some of the words, which were complaints, mainly about food. Amanda wondered what it would be like having that angry voice in her ears all day when the weather warmed up and open-window season came. She felt a twinge of resentment as she began to prepare dinner, searching among half-empty boxes for elusive equipment. She had really preferred the hectic but exciting apartment in the city. Her husband had sold her on the idea of suburban life with its peace and quiet, but that was turning out to be an empty promise.

Masatoshi came home late that evening, frazzled from negotiating an unfamiliar commute. Halfway through dinner, she asked him, "Do you know anything about those people next door?

Masatoshi heaved himself up with a grunt to refill his rice bowl. The grunt was for her, she knew. He disliked her "self-service" policy at mealtimes, but had given up lecturing her about his own mother, who, to hear him tell it, had never sat down once during his entire childhood.

"Not much. The husband is with some kind of trading company, I think." His mouth was full again almost before he had sat down.

"Someone is making a lot of noise over there. I heard them shouting all day. Somebody very old."

"Not our business." He changed the subject. "Did Mother come over today?"

"No, she didn't." Masatoshi's mother lived around the corner from their new house. That had been the main reason for the move: she was getting old, and they should be near her in case she needed anything. It was the Japanese way. How could a mere foreigner argue with that? Amanda got up to clear the table.

After about a week in the new house, Amanda emerged from her front door one cloudy morning with a bulging green trash bag. Huffing in the frosty air, she walked past the dull, decorous suburban houses to the trash enclosure, and, opening the wire door, heaved the bag inside. Her exuberant motion almost knocked over a tiny birdlike woman who had come up behind her with her own trash bag.

"Oh—*sumimasen*," Amanda murmured, but the woman answered in perky, fluent English. "Please, don't mention it." She smiled and continued, "How do you do? My name is Ishida. I think we're neighbors." Dropping her mask of Japanese politeness, Amanda smiled back. "Hello, I'm Amanda Murata."

The little woman closed the cage door and fell into step beside Amanda. They walked along, exchanging pleasantries, until Mrs. Ishida stopped, and Amanda realized that this woman lived in the House of the Yelling Old Person.

"My husband is away a lot on business," said Mrs. Ishida, continuing to speak in English as she opened her gate. "I'm a bit lonely, so I hope we'll be good friends."

"That will be nice," Amanda responded. Then, impulsively, she added, "How about some coffee?"

Mrs. Ishida didn't come in for coffee that day, but she did ring Amanda's doorbell a few mornings later, holding a wrapped box at chest level.

"I hope you don't mind. I thought we could eat these cakes together."

"Um—please come in," Amanda replied, a little startled. She opened the door and stood aside, surreptitiously whisking up a pile of laundry from the foot of the stairs and tucking it into the closet.

Soon the two were seated almost knee to knee in the small front parlor, hemmed in by the giant overstuffed sofa and chairs that Masatoshi had insisted on buying for the new house. Amanda gradually felt more at ease as Mrs. Ishida chatted lightly, praising the American coffee and the unlikely furniture. Speaking in English definitely helped. She sometimes got tired of negotiating

all the thorny obstacles of Japanese conversation. People seemed to have an inflated idea of her fluency, and she was often confused by bland statements that hinted at deeper meanings she couldn't understand. There was no need for such second-guessing now, although Mrs. Ishida's English was just as polite as her Japanese would have been, with old-fashioned phrases which made Amanda occasionally turn aside to hide a grin.

As she poured more coffee, no longer disoriented by the idea of cream cakes at nine in the morning, Amanda decided to broach the subject that was uppermost in her mind. "Do you have an elderly relative living with you?"

Mrs. Ishida jumped a little and laughed, and a few crumbs fell from her handkerchief-draped lap onto the floor. "Oh, I do apologize. I'm afraid my mother-in-law isn't accustomed to being an invalid. She never lets a minute go by without complaining about something. Can you hear her very clearly? Of course you can. I'm so sorry."

"That's quite all right," said Amanda hastily. "It's too bad she's ill. May I ask what's wrong with her?"

"She's diabetic, and recently she lost the use of her legs. She isn't really all that ill, but she does require special food and medicine, as well as all the personal attentions, of course."

"That must be difficult. Don't you have anyone to help you?"

Mrs. Ishida laughed again. It seemed to Amanda that she did a lot of laughing. "Oh, no, I can manage. In any case it's my duty to care for my husband's parents. Actually, my father-in-law is also living with us, but he's in the hospital at the moment."

"Wow."

"So you see, I can't get out as often as I'd like. It would be nice if my husband could give me a break once in a while, but you know what men are. Always working. And he's an only child, so there are no siblings to help out."

"Oh, dear." Amanda was privately appalled. "What do his parents think of you?"

"Well, they never liked me—they never thought I was good enough for their son, I suppose. It must be irksome for them to have to submit to my care." Mrs. Ishida glanced at her watch and put down her coffee cup. "I'm sorry, I have to go—it's almost time for Granny's medicine. I hope I haven't bored you! It's so good to talk in English for a while."

"Where did you learn to speak so well?" Amanda asked as she showed her guest to the door.

"I spent five years in London when I was a student. I wanted to become a confectioner—make cakes, you know. Maybe have my own shop. But instead, I met my husband. Now I buy the cakes I don't have time to make." Again the laugh. Amanda watched as Mrs. Ishida went up the path to her front door and closed it behind her with a firm click. It occurred to her that Masatoshi was also an only child.

2

As winter inched its way along, Amanda and Mrs. Ishida shared more talks over coffee and cake—always in Amanda's living room. Mrs. Ishida, who soon insisted on being called Yoko, brought different cakes every time, always from high-class shops, and was an exemplary guest; but she never invited Amanda into her own home. Maybe she felt ill at ease—maybe her house was a mess because she was busy taking care of the old lady. Amanda was a little afraid to imagine her new friend's life. She supposed Japanese women were just stronger, more capable of handling these complex family situations.

The nagging, raucous complaints continued. Amanda listened to them with half an ear as she went about her housework and prepared the lessons for the part-time English teaching she had taken on. Eventually they joined the background music of her life, as unnoticed as traffic sounds or birdsong.

Then, suddenly, one day they were gone.

That morning was cool and soft, the sun pressing against fine-grained clouds. As Amanda sat down to breakfast (Masatoshi had eaten and left for work long before) she was struck by the ringing silence. It was as though she'd gone deaf—but no, she heard the piercing whistle of a distant nightingale. She waited. There it was again, on a different note this time. The silence went on, and Amanda began to feel uneasy. She put her dishes in the sink and peeked through the window at the neighbor's house.

Just as she had made up her mind to go and ask if everything was all right, the silence was broken by the two-note blare of an ambulance, swelling to a climax and then suddenly cut off as the vehicle itself swooped into view and stopped in front of the Ishida house. Amanda stood frozen at the window as two paramedics carrying a stretcher rushed up the path and through the front door, which opened magically from inside. In no time the film was reversed and the paramedics rushed back down the path, this time carrying a burden on the stretcher. Yoko followed, looking neither left nor right, walking purposefully in spite of the huge shopping bags she carried in both hands. They all vanished into the ambulance, which erupted again in its war cry and wailed its way down the street. Going, going, gone. In the ensuing silence, the nightingale resumed its whistling.

As far as Amanda could see from her window, the funeral was mostly a succession of shiny black cars coming and going. She knew nothing about Japanese funerals, but this didn't seem to be a large one, and it was soon over. Amanda wondered if she ought to go over and knock on Mrs. Ishida's door, but her ignorance of the protocol made her shy, and she never did. Afterward, her newly awakened ears were aware of all kinds of neighborhood noises: the song of the paper recycler's truck; the whizzing of bicycles; someone's TV broadcasting the noontime news. Time passed. The air warmed up day by day; Amanda garnered a few more English students. Yoko didn't appear at her door and there were no more chats over coffee and cake.

One full-moon night in April, Masatoshi came home very late and very drunk. Startling her out of a sound sleep, he burrowed into her futon. At first he was jolly, his slurred endearments borne on a tide of whiskey-scented breath, but her lukewarm response soon had him truculently jerking at her nightdress and muttering about their honeymoon. When he finally conked out, she got up, in some pain, and trailed her blanket down the stairs, to pass a sleepless night on the living room sofa. Masatoshi banged out the door next morning with a pale, stony face and no breakfast. Amanda watched him go from the sofa, feeling very married indeed.

On a silky, silvery spring morning of rain scented with peach blossoms, Yoko again rang Amanda's doorbell with her usual smile and box of cakes. "Please forgive my long silence," she said breezily, "and many thanks for your condolences." (These had been offered, diffidently, by the Muratas at the neighbors' front door a few days after the funeral. It was the first time either of them had met the scowling, mountainous Mr. Ishida. Amanda had wondered how he and Yoko slept together, and decided that they didn't.) Amanda took her place across from her guest, the coffee and cakes between them. She wondered how to break the ice, but Yoko jumped right in with her customary cheerfulness.

"I know it's been a long time—can you forgive me? I've been so busy . . . of course you don't know about funeral customs here, do you? And I pray you'll never have to find out. So troublesome!"

"Did your mother-in-law suffer much at the end?"

"Well, I don't think so. She slipped into a coma—that's quite common among diabetics—and just stopped breathing after a few hours."

"It must feel strange now to be alone most of the time,"

Amanda heard herself say. She was immediately consumed with embarrassment—was the remark too intimate? However, Yoko seemed not to have heard. She stared into space and her voice took on a musing tone.

"She fell unconscious, yes . . . It must have been because she didn't get her medicine on time."

"What?"

Yoko looked up. "Oh, we had an argument—something about bedclothes? I don't recall—and she called me all sorts of names. Finally I got so angry, I just walked out of the room and shut the door. I peeped in there a couple of hours later—she'd simmered down, and I thought she might be in the mood to apologize . . . but she was just lying there. I thought she had fallen asleep. When I checked again a while later, I realized that she should have had her medicine long before. I guess I forgot. But she shouldn't have made me so angry."

Amanda couldn't believe her ears. Stunned, she stared at Yoko's cheerful elfin face. As if in a dream she heard Yoko continue.

"Well, I won't have time to be lonely, because my father-in-law is coming back from the hospital next week."

"What about your husband?" Amanda managed to say.

"He's in Europe. I guess he'll be in and out as usual. But please forgive me for running on like this." Yoko stood up. "I just wanted to thank you, and to tell you I hope we can resume our delightful morning chats."

They did resume them. Everything went on just as before. For a time, Amanda was a little rattled by Yoko's unrelentingly pleasant smile, but she tried to convince herself that she must have misunderstood her, as she often misunderstood Japanese people. Anyway, Amanda couldn't resist the chance to chat in her own language, so she continued to open the door to Yoko's knock a couple of times a week. Except for mentioning that her father-in-law was senile as well as bedridden, Yoko kept the conversation general. She bent enthusiastically over Amanda's modest flower garden, which was now sending up small tufts of marigolds and periwinkles.

Once, at night, Amanda caught herself gazing through the bedroom window at the house next door. She turned on impulse to Masatoshi, a humped quilt in the gloom. "Do you know what that woman, Mrs. Ishida, said to me?"

"Mf . . . not our business . . ." Seconds later he was snoring. Amanda lay awake much longer. Yoko *couldn't* have said that . . . could she?

3

Amanda stepped out of the supermarket into the glare of the shopping street, toting groceries in a heavy cloth bag. Summer in Japan! It took her breath away with its full-on, savage intensity. How could this be the same country that sheltered misty pines and soft mountain lakes, silken sleeves glimpsed in shadowed doorways and delicate flower arrangements poised on dark wooden windowsills? She always expected to come out into the sunshine and, when her eyes adjusted, find herself surrounded by dark smooth Thai bodies or the bright ruffled skirts of Mexico. The sunlight pressed down on her head. She remembered she had a hat somewhere under the groceries, and rummaged for it.

Plunking the hat on her head with a sigh of relief, Amanda saw a figure she knew a few paces away. It was Yoko, cool in linen and proceeding decorously beneath a lavender-colored parasol. They met at the pedestrian crossing.

"Yes, I'm quite busy taking care of my father-in-law," said Yoko in response to Amanda's query. "I do manage to get out for a few minutes a day to shop. It's a nice change, even though it's so hot."

Amanda was considering what to say next when the ground seemed to drop from under her. Clutching Yoko's shoulder, she saw the other woman's eyes widen as the crowd exploded with startled shouts of "Earthquake!" The traffic lights swung wildly on their wires and then abruptly blinked out. Gradually the tremor abated, and exclamations of relief were mingled with annoyed remarks about the power outage. Harassed housewives burst from darkened shops, forcing open the inoperative automatic doors. The crowd got larger, each person recounting his own experience at the top of his lungs and nobody listening.

"This way," said Yoko, and taking her friend's arm, steered her through the crush toward the welcome shade of a small park nearby. Under the trees, a jolly man was selling bottles of old-fashioned *ramune*, which he fished with red dripping hands out of ice water in a bathtub-sized cooler. Soon Amanda found herself sitting on a bench beside Yoko in the shifting dapples of shade. The fizzy lemonade tickled her tongue and drove ice-cold spikes of delicious pain into her forehead.

Yoko drained her bottle and inspected the glass marble rolling around in the bottom. Then she looked at her watch. "My goodness! Have we been here that long? I must get back." She gave the bottle to the vendor, bowed to Amanda, and clicked off down the tree-lined path, gold coins of sunlight sliding off her shoulders.

Amanda remained on the bench and watched her disappear in the crowd. The park was cool, and the way home was long. She suddenly recalled that Yoko had, without comment, looked at her watch at least three times during the few minutes they sat there; but she felt too lightheaded to think about it further.

The black cars returned to the quiet suburban street. Mr. Ishida again scowled down from his great height at the offered condolences on the death of his father. As before, a period of silence and calm ensued, with no sign of Yoko. Amanda watched the house covertly. She almost hoped that this time there would be no bland resumption of coffee and cakes in the mornings, because she had other things to think about. She was pregnant. It must have happened on that spring night of unwanted passion and whiskey fumes. This new reality occupied the center of her life, and seemed also to have galvanized her mother-in-law, who had taken to dropping by much more often than before. Masatoshi encouraged the visits, digging with gusto into the prepared foods she brought, and repeatedly remarking that "you two must have a lot to talk about now." Amanda doubted it. These people were going to squeeze her between them till there was nothing left.

One blustery autumn morning, when a high wind was blowing the leaves off the trees before they could change color, Amanda was out on the second-floor deck, her hair whipped around her head, trying to bring in the laundry before it started raining. Faintly over the roar of the wind, she heard the doorbell. The door to the balcony was at a strange angle to the stairs, and required a twist of the hips to get through. She carefully maneuvered herself through the narrow doorway and down the stairs. Yoko stood at the front door, bubbly as usual, holding her box of cakes up against her chest, covered by an expensive hand-knitted sweater Amanda had never seen before. Obviously she had something to tell. Sure enough, as soon as the coffee cups touched the table, she launched in.

"I wanted to tell you—I'm going away for a while."

"Really?" This was news indeed, given the pattern of Yoko's life up to now.

"Yes. You see, we came into a little money when my father-in-law died, and my husband said I could use some of it to spend three months in London on a refresher course. You know I've always been interested in the confectionery business"—she paused dramatically—"and I'm going to have my own shop at last! When I get back from London, it's going to happen! I have the shop all picked out—it's across town, but now that I don't have anyone to take care of at home, I can stay out as long as I like. I can even spend the night there."

Amanda stared at her neighbor's glowing face. She had heard about this dream before, but had always assumed it was a fantasy to carry Yoko through her days of thankless work. Apparently not—it was real. She felt a stab of envy, and decided on the spur of the moment to tell Yoko her own news.

"Actually, I have something to tell you too. I'm going to have a baby."

"Oh!" Yoko gave a cry of delight. "How wonderful! I hope you'll be very happy! What fun to have a baby to play with right next door!" Her tone was shrill, and she didn't quite look at Amanda, but fiddled with her coffee spoon. Amanda felt a trifle queasy.

"Well! Me with cakes, and you with a baby—we'll have a busy year!" Yoko crowed. Then she lowered her voice. "By the way, once again, thanks for your condolences. You and your husband are very kind."

Amanda blinked. "That's all right . . . I guess your father-in-law passed away pretty suddenly?"

Yoko looked up. Her eyes were wide and innocent. "Oh yes, I guess I never got to tell you what happened. Remember the day we met in town, when we had that earthquake? Well, the power outage that followed . . . I'm afraid it interfered with Grandpa's medical monitors. When I got home he was unconscious, and he died soon after. Well, Amanda-san, I must be going—my plane leaves this afternoon. Please take care of yourself." And with her birdlike smile, she was off.

Amanda gazed after her, open-mouthed, from her front step till Yoko had disappeared behind her own front door.

4

"I'm home." There was the clunk of a briefcase falling to the floor, and then Masatoshi appeared in the kitchen doorway, loosening his tie. He made straight for the refrigerator and began investigating square containers. "Yum! Rice with *matsutake!* My mother makes the best." He yanked open the door of the microwave and shoved the container in, pushing buttons. The newspapery aroma of matsutake mushrooms began to fill the kitchen. While he waited, Masatoshi eyed Amanda, who was sitting at the kitchen table, staring straight in front of her. "What's wrong with you?"

Amanda's eyes found her husband's. "She looked at her watch *before*," she muttered. "She looked at her watch *three times*."

Bing! said the microwave, as if in agreement. Masatoshi grabbed the container out with a muffled curse at the heat, got some chopsticks, and began shoveling in the brownish rice. "What are you talking about?" he said around his mouthful.

Amanda closed her eyes and felt ill. Behind her eyelids she saw a slim, brown Japanese boy laughing as he ran down a beach in Hawaii. Her husband. Where was that boy now? She said slowly, "There's something strange going on next door. Remember those two funerals?"

"Yeah."

"That lady, Mrs. Ishida, was responsible for those deaths. She practically confessed it to me in so many words."

Masatoshi's reply was sharp. "Whatever gave you that idea? You'd better be careful what you say."

Amanda's eyes flew open. "But you don't understand! She *told* me. Right in our living room. She said she refused to give the old lady her medicine, and then the old man, she deliberately delayed her return from the market while his monitors failed and he died. I was there. She was watching the time."

Masatoshi never paused in his meal. As soon as the rice was finished, he got up and started rooting around in the fridge again. He took out something with an eye-watering vinegar smell and dug in, watching her narrowly over his chopsticks. "Did you say anything about this to my mother?"

"No . . ."

"Well, don't. You're a foreigner. You have to understand, it's not our business. We don't interfere. It's the Japanese way." He finished the vinegary stuff and tossed the containers into the sink. "Anyhow, you probably just imagined the whole thing. Pregnant women have vivid imaginations, I've heard that." He grabbed a can of beer and went out. In a moment Amanda heard the splashy music and laughter of a TV game show. She stood up shakily, got a bowl, and served herself from the pot of soup she had made. Only five months pregnant and already she felt like an old woman.

As autumn deepened, and her pregnancy continued on its rather difficult course, Amanda felt as if she had been shoved into a box and the lid nailed down. Her husband had entirely ceased to listen to anything she said, and her mother-in-law nagged her constantly about her health. Were they in league against her, or was it just paranoia, as Masatoshi had said? She felt her ideas about Yoko changing as well. Her earlier sharp suspicions seemed to have faded, leaving only a tired envy of Yoko doing her refresher course in London. She missed their talks over coffee and cake. Her English classes had been dwindling as her strength did, and now she didn't have anyone to talk to at all.

One bright brisk morning she struggled up the stairs with a basket of wet laundry. As soon as she made it to the landing, she heard the front door open and the hallooing of her mother-in-law. "I'll be right there!" she called crossly. She took a moment to balance her sizable stomach in order to get through the tricky door, and that was when she looked toward the house next door and saw a full load of laundry flapping on the balcony. Yoko must have returned from her trip. Amanda was tempted to go over and knock on the door. Yoko would have lots of news, and might even invite her into the house that was now hers alone. She felt a surge of unaccustomed energy.

Amanda finished hanging up the clothes and descended the narrow staircase one slow step at a time. Her mother-in-law spied her from the kitchen, where she was unpacking yet another bag of food, and yelled out "Careful!" I'm *being* careful, Amanda thought, scowling. She stopped to catch her breath and with an enormous effort, tacked a species of smile on her face before she entered the kitchen and greeted the relentlessly cheerful old lady.

"Good morning, Mother. What have you brought us today?"

"Seasonal delicacies—chestnut rice and boiled vegetables with tofu." The mother set the containers down and regarded Amanda critically. "You look very thin and tired. You need to take better care of yourself. That's my grandchild you're carrying! Aren't you eating my good food?"

"Yes, I am," Amanda lied. (The truth was, she couldn't get her mother-in-law's food down at all.) "Masatoshi always shares it with me."

The mother's brow wrinkled. "When you talk about my son to me, you must say Masatoshi-*san*," she said in a pinched, disapproving tone.

"Sorry. I'm just a bit out of sorts this morning. I should

probably take a walk later." This would be a good excuse to visit Yoko. Dully, she realized she had become rather good at lying.

"Good idea—exercise is important," was the bossy reply. "Well, Amanda-san, I'll be going. I have a lot to do today. See you tomorrow. I'm certainly looking forward to this."

"Excuse me?"

"I guess Masa-kun didn't tell you. What a bad boy! He invited me to stay with you two until the baby is born. I'm moving in tomorrow. I know you'll appreciate the help—you can't take care of your husband properly in your condition." Suddenly Amanda's expression of total shock seemed to penetrate the mother's self-absorption. "Don't worry, it's the Japanese way. *Your* mother can't help you, obviously, all the way across the ocean." With a bray of laughter, the mother took her leave.

As soon as she was out of sight, Amanda left her house and waddled rapidly up the path to the Ishidas' front door. She imagined how good it would be to see a friendly face as she waited for a response to her knock.

The door swung open and Amanda took a breath to say hello to Yoko, but instead a tiny elderly lady stood there, her eyes wide at the sight of a foreigner on the doorstep. For a moment they gazed at each other, their faces mirroring exactly the same thought: Who could this be? "*Ah, gomen kudasai,*" stammered Amanda. "I'm from next door . . ."

The old eyes regarded her in utter perplexity.

"Next door," Amanda repeated helplessly. "Is Yoko-san at home?"

There was a flurry in the room beyond, and Yoko suddenly appeared, grasping the door with her hand. "Amanda-san!" she stammered. "What a pleasant surprise. Just one moment." She took the old lady by the shoulders and guided her gently but firmly back into the house, nudging the door shut with her foot. In a few seconds it clicked open again and Yoko stood there, her old smile once more in place.

"My friend, it is good to see you. How have you been? I see the baby is growing!"

"How are you, Yoko? When did you get back?"

Yoko looked a little embarrassed. "About two weeks ago. I'm sorry I haven't been able to come over and chat with you."

"I have missed our chats," Amanda admitted. "So, how's the cake shop? Is it up and running yet?"

"The cake shop?" Yoko seemed suddenly vague, turning the words over slowly. "Oh, I'm afraid I don't have time for that."

Amanda felt deflated. She realized that the thought of Yoko fulfilling her dream had been a vital support for her over the past months. "What happened? And who is that lady?"

Yoko glanced quickly over her shoulder, as if she thought the old woman might be sneaking up on her. "Oh, that's my mother."

"Your mother is visiting you? How nice." With a sudden stab of longing, Amanda had a vision of her own mother, brisk and gray-haired, sitting down to cards with her friends, driving to quilting lessons in her little car.

"Yes, she's moved in with me, as she can no longer take care of herself—she's very confused, you know." Yoko gazed at Amanda, lowered her voice, and murmured, "But I don't think she'll be here long."

Amanda never knew how she got back to her own house. Her senses seemed dreamy and crystal clear at the same time. She packed a small bag, made a couple of phone calls, and booked a plane ticket online. Just before stepping out the door to the waiting taxi, she turned back and hastily scrawled a note which she left on the kitchen table.

Dear Masatoshi-san,
Please tell your mother there are clothes drying on the balcony.
And tell her to be careful on the stairs.   —Amanda

Three Village Tales

1. The Reluctant Tea Teacher

BOOM, ba bap bap BOOM, da da da da da BOOM, ba bap bap BOOM . . .

A sudden flood of amplified sound, up from the floor, in from the walls. Seated on their demure little bamboo stools in a row, the students tried to hide their winces behind a ripple of chatter. Mrs. Miyazaki, whose turn it was to make tea, stared bemusedly at the array of utensils in front of her. Conversation died, and four pairs of middle-aged-lady eyes swiveled to Sensei.

BOOM, ba bap bap BOOM . . . Sensei felt the pressure of attention, looked up, and seamlessly, gently, mentioned the next step in the ritual. Mrs. Miyazaki jerked into motion with an embarrassed half-smile; the watching students relaxed; the boom-ba-boom went on, oblivious.

Sensei didn't try to talk herself out of it any more—she was stupefied with boredom from years of sitting in this room in the garishly renovated village hall, under glaring fluorescents, teaching tea to complacent country ladies. They made tea as though washing the dinner dishes, clinking and clunking their way through the ritual, fiercely focused on getting the order right, unable to lift their minds enough to inject any beauty into their spacing or timing. Meanwhile, the watching students chatted about their ailing mothers-in-law, pickle recipes, an old dog's incontinence. And right next door—right next door!—in a masterpiece of bad scheduling, the neighborhood karaoke group wailed through the same boom-ba-boom songs time after time, week after week, with a rudeness as careless as it was unconscious, drowning out the delicate hissing of the tea kettle and the subdued clink of utensils.

Mrs. Miyazaki finished making the tea and placed the tea bowl in exactly the wrong place on the stand beside her, then faced forward again. Sensei glided off her stool with the unobtrusiveness of long practice, picked up the tea bowl, and cupping it affectionately, carried it back to her seat. Murmuring the ritual apology to her neighbor, she brought the warm, rough bowl to her lips. Ah! The hot astringent foamy liquid flooded her mouth. This was the only moment in the whole lesson that she felt was worthwhile. She even forgot the relentless thumping of the karaoke. Moving gently and with gratitude, she replaced the bowl at the student's right hand, in exactly the right place. She reseated herself, savoring the smooth rise of the caffeine into her head, the sudden pounding of the heart, the intensity of vision. Thank goodness it was the custom at these lessons to serve tea to the teacher first! She had about half an hour of artificial wakefulness until the sooty dust bunnies of boredom descended again.

The ritual continued without any further hitches. The only problem with the caffeine was that it intensified the combination of the karaoke and the ladies' prattle into a finely calibrated torture. Which was worse, Sensei mused, as she automatically murmured the litany of set responses—death by suffocation in boredom, or death by excruciating assaults on the senses? Ruefully she recalled that the Zen monks had originally adopted tea drinking centuries ago as an antidote to sleepiness during meditation. After all these years, the tea ceremony itself had acquired the power to induce degrees of drowsiness undreamed of by those simple monks of yore.

Nearing the end, the student lifted the elegant long-handled bamboo ladle off the kettle and clunked it into the cold-water container. Sensei's absolutely invisible wince had taken years to perfect. Her mind wandered through the coming lesson—the peccadilloes of the next student, the amount of water remaining in the kettle, the customary seasonal words to describe the bamboo tea scoop.

And then, a miracle happened. Both the boom-ba-boom and the mindless chatter suddenly ceased at exactly the same moment, leaving only the susurration of the water gently boiling in the kettle, a sound the classical poets described as "wind in the pines." As the student poured the cold water into the kettle, the water's hiss was stilled and a huge, broad, grateful silence spread through the room like a living thing, touching the ears of all within it in a benediction of nothingness. The universal spirit of everything flashed out like a diamond. Time stood still. Dazzled, Sensei caught her breath.

Too soon, much too soon, everyday life reasserted itself. The karaoke resumed in a different rhythm, sweeping away all thoughts of universal oneness; the ladies took up their conversation where they had left off; Mrs. Miyazaki bumbled out of the room. Sensei resumed her meticulous examination of the slightly reddened knuckles neatly folded in her lap. She found herself remembering a Zen aphorism learned in her student days: "Before enlightenment—drawing water and carrying wood. After enlightenment—drawing water and carrying wood." Was it enough? It would have to be. Sensei looked up to acknowledge the bow of the next student and set herself to do it all over again.

2. Revenge

I hate my dad.

Every day of my life when I was a kid, he used to beat me. Some days it was just a tap across the face or a box on the ear. Other days it was a real drubbing around the shoulders and back, with his fists or anything handy—a piece of wood, a rake handle. My dad used to be really strong. He was a builder. Carried heavy ceramic roof tiles and installed them all over the village. He had huge muscles in his arms. I used to go around with big bruises all over me.

His voice is really loud, too, and he never shuts up. All the time he was hitting me in my boyhood, he was yelling. I think kids' hearing must be more sensitive than adults'. His yelling made my head hurt. Some days I didn't know which hurt most— my head or my body.

I'm big now, I'm a grown man, so he doesn't beat me—that's changed, at least—but he still yells, and I can't stand it. Sometimes my head hurts so bad it feels like it's going to explode. That's how it feels tonight. He just got through yelling at me because I forgot to bring the sake back from town. So what? He drinks too much anyway.

Tonight's the night. I'm going to pay him back.

I think it's dark enough now. He's watching TV with my mother. I hate her too, for letting him do those things to me. But it's him I really hate. Wait till he sees what I did!

Sneak out the back door with the kerosene can. Boy, it's heavy. Don't forget the matches. Don't turn on the light in case they notice. Sneak down the lane in the dark, all the way to the shed where he parks his precious truck. He won't let me drive it. I have to go everywhere by bike. I hate him.

Squeeze past the piles of roof tiles. Open the truck door in the dark. It smells like him—his revolting breath, his clothes. My head is throbbing. Lift the can and slosh the kerosene all over the seat. Now the match. Whooo! Look at those flames. I feel the heat on my face. Shut the door and sneak into Mr. Sato's yard next door, hide behind the fence.

The fire gets bigger and bigger. The light shines through the chinks of the shed. I hear the fire roaring. What's that? Another sound. Someone has seen the fire and called the volunteers. It's the siren on the big red fire engine they keep down by the school. It's coming this way.

Hey—what are you doing? Let me go! Hey, Sato-san, let me go!

Two Years Later

It didn't work. All the planning, all the guts it took to set dad's truck on fire, and what it got me was a jail sentence for arson. It's not fair. No one ever asked me why I did it. No one ever thought that dad might be to blame. That dumb Mr. Sato caught me and they figured out I did it, I don't know how. The truck didn't even burn much. Just the seats. The firefighters got there before the fire reached the gas tank. I was hoping for a big explosion. Oh, how I was hoping the whole shed would go up— dad's livelihood gone. But it didn't work. My head hurts worse than ever. It never stops now.

They sent me home—but I won't live here anymore. They can't make me.

Only, where can I go?

Actually . . . why should I leave? This is a perfectly good house.

Dad's out shopping with Mom in his new truck. Fire insurance. Holy hell. He gets everything and I get nothing. Well, that changes now.

The official seals and bankbooks with his name—out the front door with them. They land on the path. I don't want to leave him with nothing. I want him to live and think about what he did and be miserable every day.

Lock the doors on the inside. Move the furniture—the big wooden kitchen cabinet, the chests, the bureaus—up against the doors and windows. Barricade the place. I'm strong now, myself—as strong as he used to be. He's an old man now, he can't do anything.

Let him live in the shed, him and mom. They won't ever get

into this house again. This is my home now. The son takes over from the father, that's the rule, and it starts now.

Oh, my head.

3. The Outsider

Old Tatsuki trudged home, hefting his weed whacker, his work clothes sticking to him in itchy, sweaty patches. His shoulders bowed under the relentless summer sun. He was tired and depressed.

The argument in the graveyard still rang in his ears. The audacity of Mrs. Nakamura! He had done more work than anyone else, but instead of adulation, angry faces had been turned toward him. Instead of receiving gratitude, he had been accused of unfairness.

It was just by chance that Tatsuki had heard of Mr. Kimura's decision to come early to the yearly grave cleaning. Mr. Kimura, a fellow member of the temple, had another obligation later in the day, so he wanted to get the cleaning finished before that. Tatsuki idolized Mr. Kimura and his mother, Akiko. Her husband, now deceased, had always cleaned the graveyard before anyone else arrived. This, to Tatsuki, was the essence of belonging to the village—to go above and beyond the call of duty. The more work one did, the more prestige one could accumulate. Eager to appear as if he belonged as well, he had rushed through his breakfast and joined Mr. Kimura.

Arriving at the graveyard at six o'clock instead of the seven o'clock agreed upon by the temple members, he and Mr. Kimura revved up their weed whackers and set to work. The shoulder-high grass fell in swathes before their roaring machines. Step by step, they cut their way down the forest path, and gradually the old stone graves came into view. Once they had cleared the central space, they turned off the machines and gathered armloads of grass and dwarf bamboo, slinging them aside into the undergrowth. It took half an hour, but the whole public area was finished. Their work done, Tatsuki and Mr. Kimura exchanged glances of self-congratulation, and wiping their faces, slogged up the now-spotless path toward the road.

Tatsuki was an old man. He had a lot in common with the other old men of the village—their aches and pains, their home lives. But he was an outsider, and he knew it. He had not been born here, had not even lived here as a child, but had come about fifteen years before to take over his ancestral house from his ailing mother. His own children had never lived here either, and his wife was from a completely different area of Japan. Since his mother's passing, he had fought a constant uphill battle not to be regarded as a *yoso-mono* (person from elsewhere). He took on the village duties as they came around, and did them to the best of his ability. He presented himself at the temple for the various ceremonies and cleaning sessions. He attended the drinking sessions and dinners, listening carefully for every scrap of local information, gauging the relative importance of each man in the local hierarchy. He tried with all his might to fit in. But somehow, inside his head at least, nothing was ever enough. He was always bumping up against some situation where he was reminded, wordlessly but forcibly, that he was an outsider and always would be.

Tatsuki had decided that fitting in was pretty much a matter of finding the strongest man and doing whatever he did. This seemed to be the quickest way to be accepted, on the coattails of a stronger person. He himself was not strong. He had never even attracted the attention of the bullies at school, but had always just blended in. He wanted to blend in here, to settle down in a niche in the corner, out of everyone's way but indisputably accepted as one of them. So, when an opportunity like this graveyard cleaning presented itself, he eagerly followed Mr.

Kimura, who had a local reputation for strength that he had inherited from his father and grandfather.

Arriving at the road, Tatsuki saw that Mr. Uemura, the temple officer, had just arrived with Mrs. Nakamura to begin work. What a surprise they would have when they discovered everything already done! Especially Mrs. Nakamura! Now that woman was a true outsider, who was not only from elsewhere in Japan but from a real foreign country, Australia, and who had married into the village thirty years before. She was an outsider that actually looked and acted like an outsider—not a hardworking chameleon like him. Tatsuki had often been startled at her arrogance and don't-care attitude. Though she did the work and participated in everything, she didn't seem to feel in her heart the need to belong. Well, this time he would show her the reality—the kind of effort that was necessary to really fit in here.

Tatsuki had been seen by other temple members leaving in Mr. Kimura's company, both of them tired and sweaty from work. There was no doubt that they had worked shoulder to shoulder. Whatever prestige Mr. Kimura gained from doing all the work would be his as well. He was satisfied.

Some minutes later, Tatsuki returned to the graveyard, ostensibly to explain to Mr. Uemura that he had joined Mr. Kimura in going to work early, but actually to soak up some of the gratitude he was sure would come his way. Mr. Uemura and Mrs. Nakamura were standing in the center of the public area, deep in conversation. A couple of other members were in the background. "I just thought I'd come early and do a bit extra today," Tatsuki said modestly, coming up to them.

"Mrs. Nakamura doesn't like it," responded Mr. Uemura.

Flabbergasted, Tatsuki turned toward Mrs. Nakamura, who was wearing her usual expression of harsh disagreement. "I expected a little more gratitude, after working so hard," he said.

What followed he was unable to understand. After protesting that she was indeed grateful—an obvious lie—she proceeded to tell Tatsuki that she thought it was unfair for him to take all the work when the others had arrived on time, in good faith, ready to do their share. Unfair? What did that have to do with it? She seemed actually angry that she had been cheated out of the opportunity to work.

"You have been here longer than I have. You have been here for thirty years. You ought to know how things work around here," Tatsuki pronounced. He looked around at the others for acknowledgment, but they were expressionless, evidently hoping for an end to this uncomfortable argument. Did no one agree with him? Was no one going to show gratitude? He swung around and left.

Tatsuki arrived home and stripped off his sweaty clothes. He couldn't understand it. Everyone knew that prestige, climbing up the ladder of the hierarchy in the village, was the most important thing in life. This new social business of "equality" and "consideration" and "sharing" was a bunch of poppycock. It was all about who was strongest, who was at the top of the heap.

And yet Mrs. Nakamura, the foreigner, didn't seem to think so. Instead of smiling politely and thanking him for doing so much work, her eyes lowered, as a proper woman would, she had looked him in the face and told him exactly what she thought. She was in a weak position—she was someone who would never belong, no matter how hard she tried. But this didn't seem to bother her. Was it a Western thing? She had an air of not caring whether she belonged or not. Yet somehow, without any machinations at all, she seemed to have managed to put into words exactly what the other temple members were thinking. Otherwise they surely would have shouted her down.

Well, she would do whatever she wanted—she always had. He wondered why she bothered to show up for these village activities at all. Did she have some other motive, unrelated to the pursuit of power? No, he couldn't understand it. But his morning was spoiled, and the prestige he had imagined flowing toward him had somehow melted away. Once again he had to start climbing that mountain of belonging. He went to the outside sink and ran some water to wash his face and hands.

Rachel and Leah

My name is Rachel.

I'm trudging over beige winter grass under a tumultuous sky. Wool from my hat tickles my eyebrows, wool from my scarf is damp and cold on my cheek. Wind pushes at my back. Cold arms, cold legs, eyes tearing up, nose running. I prospect in my pocket for the wad of tissues I always carry on winter walks. A mountain dusted with snow looms in the distance across the rice fields. The houses cramped between the mountain and the fields are like the insignificant buildings in old Chinese paintings.

My mind wanders. I am thinking about making over a vest I created about ten years ago from a Guatemalan skirt. The vest turned out too big and barrel-shaped, even for my pudgy figure. I remember wearing the skirt to a historical theme park many years ago. People stared, as they always do. I suppose the vibrant multicolored stripes were a bit loud, but still it was me, the foreigner, they were staring at—the clothes were secondary.

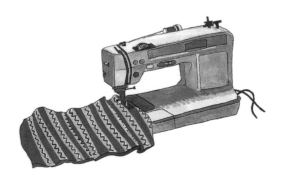

Those houses barely visible through stinging snow: they look small, but the people in them are life-size. That's my village, the one I have lived in for thirty years. Once I was mysterious, unpredictable. Now, though, the people who live in those houses think they have my number. Whatever mystery I possess is no longer worth the trouble of figuring out, if it ever was.

Beneath the white metal bridge, the stream above the weir ripples in the wind so it seems to be flowing backwards. Black rags of crows sail past overhead. I pass under eerily whistling power lines strung across the sky; I turn the corner and the wind hits a different part of my body. I'm almost home. Should I start work on that vest today?

Later the same evening, I walk the aisles of the neon-lit hardware store in search of something to deter moles in the vegetable patch. Not poison, I don't want poison. The place is almost deserted. A couple of heavily bundled elderly men, one clutching a bag of dog

food and the other a length of pipe, wait at the cash register. I can't find what I want. They only have poison. I step outside. Snow is falling from a dishwater sky, and the day is closing down as I drive up the road toward home. The wind roughhouses across the fields and buffets my little truck. Snow slants across my headlight beams, falling and falling, always more and more.

I park the truck in the garage and lug my groceries down the lane and up the stone steps to my front door. I hear the complaints of cats kept waiting too long for their dinner. I negotiate the pitch-dark hallway (familiar as my own throat), scuff off my shoes, and enter the kitchen, flipping on lights and shedding outerwear. The house is quiet and cold as a tomb.

Later I sit at my heated table, blanket over my knees, kerosene stove hissing softly at my back. The room smells like peanut butter cookies—I have just made a batch to send to my son and his wife. My solitary dinner, vegetarian cutlets and a stir-fry with aspara-gus, is over. I've washed the dishes. There aren't very many dishes when I'm alone.

I feel the house around me, centuries old, its bones ache. Yet it is also like a child. It misses me and is glad when I get home and turn on the heater. It depends on me. This dependence weighs a ton; it is as heavy as the antiquated roof, thousands of tiles poised above my head. If there was an earthquake right now I wouldn't have a chance. Everything would just slide to the ground with a rattle and a roar, right on top of me. I'd be buried.

I pack the box for my son, the cookies and a few other items. I wonder what his wife will think of the things I've packed. She doesn't know me. Even my son doesn't know me. They all think they know me, they think they have me pinned down, just another slightly troublesome older woman. They think it's all right to stop thinking about me.

They don't know, because I haven't told them. I am someone else now.

Rachel had a lot of free time, especially at this season when the garden mostly slept. She led a solitary life, with her husband frequently away on business trips (his company was squeezing the last drops of use out of him before retirement). City life was remote, her few close friends separated from her by both space and money.

It was a bad time of year to be alone. Jackets, bedsocks, and woollen hats were her constant companions. She breathed the inside-the-airplane fug of burning kerosene, planning her day around the heaters which would have to be turned on in advance to take the chill off whatever room she wanted to sit in next. Everything she did felt like busywork: sorting cupboards, little bits of handcraft, even her beloved painting. She paced the dark rooms of her big old house like a tiger in a cage. The world outside was beautiful—big skies, powdery snow, glinting diamond dust in the air—but it was all cold.

Rachel knew that winter was her worst time. She hated cold and darkness. The sunlit scenes of her childhood in another, warmer country seemed far away. How had she ended up in this house, whose cave-like interior meant she had to burn lights all day long, whose high ceilings commandeered all the heat leaving the human beings shivering below, whose ancient wooden floors had actual daylight shining up from between the boards?

She was dying for spring, for a riot of bright flowers to wake up her eyes after all this monochrome. She would be busy in spring. She would have her garden, although it increasingly seemed like unremitting work disguised as a worthwhile pastime. Recently the garden had been disappointing. Most of the vegetables she had planted back in autumn had not yet yielded anything edible, even now in early March. They just sat there, tiny round bobbles of Brussels sprouts, cold hard broccoli two inches across. What had she done wrong this time? Gardens are forgiving places, there is always another chance next year, but forgiveness is the final step. Before that you have to endure the sins of omission, the mistakes, the despair, the wasted hours of work. She sometimes wondered if the forgiveness, the next chance, was really worth it. Spring and autumn were beautiful, but she seldom got a chance between chores to take a breath and notice the beauty of cherry blossoms or red leaves. And summer was one long hothouse of raging sunshine, storms that knocked over the garden plants, and bugs, bugs, bugs. Days of standing in the kitchen with a fan blowing on her legs, cooking up yet another batch of tomato sauce. A freezer stuffed to the gills with chopped beans and carrots and peppers—and who would eat it all?

So much work, and increasingly, so little reward.

How does change happen?

At what point do we decide we don't have to ask permission?

Between one bite of breakfast granola and the next, between one dish slotted into the dish rack and the next, between one sleeping breath and the next? Who knows?

I'm changing. It's like a flood that sneaks up on me unawares, so that before I know it I'm sitting up to my ankles in water. There's no putting all that water back where it came from. The out-of-control time is coming.

I sit in my "office," the only room in the house I feel is truly mine. Glass above, glass on three sides, this is one room where I don't have to burn lights all day. A nice big worktable and a comfy chair. Good vibrations of color and light and silence. Is it any wonder I spend most of my waking life in here? Yet I feel the chill of that water around my ankles, even in this beloved place.

I need to take stock and figure out where I've been before I can tell where I'm going. But I'm going somewhere; I can't stay here. My real self is pushing through the veneer of my life as wife and mother and neighbor. I feel myself coming to the surface—and that is a person whose existence is a mystery to everyone, including me.

I came here as a wife. Even the first time I visited, I knew that this would be the place I would live as a wife—I actually wished for it so hard that I made it come true. And I got the whole package, including the parts I couldn't know about beforehand. As well as the beauty of the countryside, I got the small-mindedness of the neighbors, who were so insulated in their tiny lives that they couldn't reach out to a stranger. As well as the gorgeous old house, I got the carping lectures of my mother-in-law, who was secretly thrilled to have an unusual daughter-in-law to give her status among her friends, but who still tried with all her might to make me into a typical Japanese wife. (If she succeeded, the kudos would go to her, a Japanese Henry Higgins.) As well as the clean air and the good water and the quiet days, I got the insidious time-theft of school and neighborhood and temple, the incomprehensible expectations that bled the heart out of me and left a performing monkey, dancing desperately to rhythms I couldn't feel, making one mistake after another and trying so hard to belong. Will this placate them? All right, how about this? The real me was driven deep underground and sedated into a Sleeping Beauty limbo.

I've learned to act this way, and the people around me no longer see me as a threat to the precious security of their lives. They no longer see me at all. That's why their lives are going to change too, when this flood that is coming finally breaks out. Not the insidious little tickling of the ankles but the raging tide.

The first one to feel the force of the flood is going to be Naohiro.

Saturday evening at the railway station. Rachel leaned against the timetable noticeboard, jingled her car keys in her pocket, and yawned. Tonight she was picking Naohiro up after another extended business trip. She always took him to the station and picked him up when he traveled, in order to have the use of his rented parking spot when he was away, but it did mean long drives to the station at all hours.

They saw each other at the same moment. It was something that happened when you had been married over thirty years.

He was one of the last to come out, struggling with his unruly, oversized bags, and his face was a combination of ecstasy and exhaustion. The ecstasy was for her, but so was the exhaustion. With his eyes turned sideways to see who would be looking, he accepted her hug reluctantly.

Walking with him to the car, she glanced at his familiar face, drawn down and immobile with tiredness. He looked so old after these trips. He loved traveling and meeting people, loved navigating and poring over maps, loved taking photographs and picking up odd little souvenirs; but it was getting to be too much for him, he was almost sixty. Rachel was almost sixty as well, but lately she felt as if she would burst with all the life that was inside her. She had noticed that in spite of menopause, or perhaps because of it, at a certain age many women took on a new lease of life, while their men dwindled and sank into complaining helplessness. Men sometimes seemed to hate older women; perhaps it was because they were jealous of their strength.

Home again, he came to her for his "real" hug in the kitchen while she made tea and looked over the things he had brought her, usually food items she had requested. They chatted about village news, while her mind grappled with the knowledge that yes, he was home for another few weeks, yes, he would require lunches packed at five a.m. before he left on his insanely long commute, yes, he would infuriate her with obliviousness and micro-management. Another time of adjustment to him had begun.

That night Naohiro fell immediately into the sleep of profound exhaustion. Rachel shoved the cat over to give herself more room, and shoved his knee over onto his side for good measure, gazing at the dim gray square of window that was the only defining feature of the pitch-black room. Her sleep was always disturbed the first few nights after he came home.

She knew that now she would slip once more into The Role: the sharp, wise-cracking "noisy wife" (his words), combined with the service—always, the service. What Naohiro wanted, in effect, was The Little Woman. Actually, he wanted two women. Because of his upbringing, at certain times he wanted a typical Japanese wife, someone he could take for granted, slumping in his chair as he waited for the meal to be prepared even when they had both been working hard—sometimes shoulder to shoulder—all day. At other times he wanted a colorful foreigner, whose outbursts he could enjoy watching as though she were a fireworks display. Someone he could try his sexist comments on, waiting for her explosive reaction to his little-boy misbehavior, although lately she couldn't seem to summon the energy.

Naohiro was a good husband. He brought home a nice pay-check, gave her carte blanche in money matters, didn't drink, smoke or run around on her, often washed the dishes, obliged with every handyman project she suggested. She was sure there was a true relationship, true camaraderie and concern, under all these games of his, but sometimes it was difficult to find.

Am I being too hard on him?

Am I being too hard on my whole life?

Should I just shut up and be satisfied with this? I know he's satisfied, because I'm still physically here, which is mostly what he wants. If only I could sustain The Role, there would be nothing to rock the complacent little boat of his life. How much like all these other villagers he is, after all—how much like his mother he is! Brags about my strangeness to impress his friends, but also longs to make me over to his own specifications.

He does brag, I know he does. He talks about me to his associates, who all say how eager they are to meet me. He doesn't under-stand my creativity, my quirkiness, my inquiring mind, my insane productivity—so why does he get to parade them all over the place, while I stay here like a piece of furniture that he's glad to sit on when he comes home? He brags about our marriage too. Says we never fight. Well, it's true, but only because I can't get him to engage. Anyway, I hate fighting, and so does he; we both had enough of family tumult as children, and we both swore that would not be the case with us. Only what am I supposed to do with my tumult now?

If those people could see us as we really are, they'd know the truth, which is that he has had my reins in his hand, exactly like a horse's bridle, for years, and he has been able to make me do anything by pulling on them. But my own participation in this is draining away. The acting persists, the "noisy wife" role, the wild animal tamed. But it's becoming more and more of an act. Does he really not notice that? Does he not see that, lately, I am standing to the side, maybe even looking the other way?

I lie and listen to his snores. Silently, I whisper: I'm someone else now. You don't know me. You don't know the person I've become.

Rachel sat in her office in her pajamas, the early morning light washing over her, her coffee at her side, her cats on her lap, the space heater ticking gently beside her. The insights that had been swirling around were coming home to roost, and she needed to sit still to let them land.

This was what it came down to. She had married Japan, lock, stock, and barrel. Japan, in microcosm, was Naohiro. Japan had its own ideas about what was good and worthy of respect, and women and foreigners were far down on the list. Therefore, they were far down on the list for Naohiro as well, even though unconsciously. To go that far against his upbringing was beyond him. His mother had been an angry woman trapped in an arranged marriage, hemmed in on all sides by The Way Things Were; therefore it was natural to him that his own wife should feel angry and hemmed-in. It was his only experience of what being a wife meant. Perhaps inevitably, he saw only his own version of her, and whatever didn't fit into that version was ignored, or subject to his manipulation. For him, she was ever and always Wife 1.0, constantly needing to be tinkered with. This thought produced a snort of laughter, even as she contemplated the bleak truths presenting themselves one by one.

When they were first married, Naohiro loved her because they had good sex, and the surprising, foreign parts of her were fascinating; but now that he was older, he no longer had the energy for exoticism. He now put up with her in the hope that this high-maintenance woman, this unmanageable "noisy wife," would finally become the supreme comfort dispenser that he, as a Japanese man, had the right to expect in his marriage. That would be his reward in old age for all his forbearance.

In a way it was like the story of Rachel and Leah in the Bible. The guy, whatever his name was (interesting that her brain couldn't cough up that detail), really wanted Rachel for his wife, but her folks wouldn't allow it. So he married her sister Leah instead, as an interim measure, in hopes of getting his hands on Rachel later on. Naohiro had married Leah, hoping to get Rachel—except in this case, they were the same woman.

Rachel considered this analogy. Had anyone ever asked the Rachel in the Bible if she even wanted to be married to what's-his-name? (Or Leah either, for that matter?) It seemed that Naohiro was getting to the age when he expected his lifelong dreams to start showing up. He wanted Leah to turn into Rachel. He was ready for the noisy wife he had endured all these years to morph into the soft, pliable, comforting Japanese wife he had always secretly wanted. Well, that wasn't going to happen. Her name might be Rachel, but she was having none of it.

If the truth be told, she didn't want to be a noisy wife, or a pliable Japanese wife either. What she wanted, in her heart of hearts, was to be what she truly was, and to have that be all right. And, sadly, she didn't think Naohiro was capable of seeing this. His dream wife, that mythical woman whose vision he had cherished all these years, was too etched in stone ever to change. But Rachel herself was now changing at a fantastic clip.

With a sigh, Rachel finished her coffee, dumped the cats off her lap, and went to get dressed. She had now officially graduated from Japan and from her old life. The people around her, Naohiro included, could try to force her back; they could ask about dead-and-gone hobbies, or her children, or whatever they thought was currently occupying her mind. They could try to make her continue to be the person that she had abandoned around the latest corner of her life. But she couldn't go backward, even for Naohiro. She had to move forward, wherever life took her.

My name is Rachel.

Once I was a crass, loud, ignorant foreigner. I had no idea of the infinite nuances of society in this place called Japan. Then, gradually, as I learned more, I started to wear the mask and actually to love it, to feel euphoria, when I edged toward Doing the Right Thing and earned a small, fragile feeling of belonging. I wore the mask with my husband too, and maybe that was a mistake, because it allowed him to dream about what might be.

I found myself trapped between these two personas—the foreigner who could never fit in and the would-be Japanese who might one day, possibly, fit in. What I didn't realize was that my fitting in was meaningless. The idea of it had no substance. That's why I have, with stupefying suddenness, come to a place where I can throw off this need to fit in, as easily as a piece of clothing. My Guatemalan vest, for instance. No need any more to worry that it doesn't fit and try to make it over. Chalk it up to experience and move on. There are a lot of other vests out there, waiting to be made.

What's ahead? I'm not sure. But one thing I know: there will be honesty there.

The Mad Kyoto Shoe Swapper

1

S ummer was the best time of year for shoe-swapping. In spring, Kyoto buzzed with beginnings—the first day of school, the first day of work; and autumn was alive with alert, sharp-eyed students and academics walking briskly through the precincts of the temples, stimulated by the fiery trees and the spanking clean, crisp air. But when the days sweltered and steamed, people trickled around in a daze, fanning themselves inattentively, until they could plunge into the next haven of air conditioning. Kyoto slept in summer, everyone knew that. It was too hot to do anything else.

A huge hillside temple, drowsing at noonday, its slanted gray roofs shimmering. In the purplish shade of the portico, a sign with the message "No Shoes Allowed" stood at the foot of ancient wooden steps that had been polished slick by millions of stocking feet. Six or eight pairs of shoes were neatly lined up against the bottom step—their owners had left them here while they explored the high, cool rooms of the temple.

Into this deserted space, enter Jiro, the Mad Kyoto Shoe Swapper. Youngish, black-haired, black-clad, unobtrusive as a beetle, he scuttled across the temple forecourt and ducked into the portico.

Jiro gazed up with an interested air at the complicated joinery of the wooden ceiling high above. After a moment he turned his back to the steps and shuffled off his shoes so that they faced outward. He glanced nonchalantly down at the row of shoes, then mounted the steps and disappeared through the wide doorway. Five minutes later he returned and walked purposefully away without a backward glance. But this time the shoes he put on were not the ones he had taken off.

Anyone who happened to notice Jiro would have said he was just a student, head full of equations and girls, taking in a temple on his lunch break from a summer job nearby. But Jiro was not a student, and no one could have imagined the contents of his head. At this moment his whole being was transfixed by the beautiful, mysterious otherness of the strange shoes, the places where they rubbed and the places where they yielded. He hardly spared a thought for the shoes he had left behind, which of course were not "his" shoes either—he had swapped them at another temple a couple of weeks previously. He strode on, sweating lightly, the sun scorching his black hair.

2

Jiro's hobby had begun by accident. Three years before, on one of his solitary walks through the city, he had visited a temple with a storehouse converted into a minute art gallery. After taking in the exhibit of black-and-white photographs, he had absent-mindedly put on the wrong shoes at the exit. His own shoes had been rather uncomfortable anyway, so he was already a hundred paces down the path before he noticed his mistake. Retracing his steps, he heard raised voices, and peeped round the corner of the building to see a foreigner flapping his hands and fussing in English at a gaping young priest. Obviously he was complaining that his shoes were missing. Jiro was fascinated and terrified by the flamboyantly angry gestures of the foreigner. It was several minutes before he plucked up the courage to step forward.

The foreigner had ranted at him, half angry and half relieved. This gave Jiro nightmares for a few days, but then the theatrical possibilities of the situation dawned on him. He began to visit temples frequently, and to look for shoes that resembled his own. If the coast was clear, he would put them on, walk briskly away around the nearest corner, and watch to see what his victim would do. He never returned the shoes again. The unfolding drama was just too thrilling to interrupt—the priceless "What now?" look on the faces, the dismayed conferring with friends, the scribbling of addresses, the apologies of the priests. Once the show was over, he just walked away.

After a few successful swaps, and some very entertaining moments, Jiro's enjoyment of the drama gave way to a more interior pleasure. He began to notice the feel of the shoes he had taken. He always walked everywhere—Kyoto was a splendid town to walk in—and there was an indescribable satisfaction in the way these strange shoes, weird and uncomfortable at first, gradually altered until they fitted him so perfectly that they were unnoticeable. He concentrated fiercely on this transition, from the moment his feet slid into the strange shoes until the moment he began to be bothered by their familiarity. It was then that he began to think about another swap.

Jiro had fine-tuned his hobby over the three years he had been shoe-swapping. He was very good at it. He had never once been caught, and he saw no reason why he should not go on indefinitely, as long as he kept to his rules:

(1) Concentrate on one style and color of shoe. Jiro always swapped black sports shoes, which were the most common of all, and he chose shoes that were approximately as worn as the ones he already had. Swapping for brand-new shoes was too risky, and what was the point of swapping for worse ones?

(2) Don't swap too frequently. Jiro limited his swaps to once every two or three weeks, and he never hit the same temple

twice. This was easy to do, as temples and shrines in Kyoto numbered well over a thousand, and many of them had the same ad hoc arrangement—shoes were left outside, with no lockers or supervision of any kind.

(3) Don't call attention to yourself, speak to no one, and never spend more than five minutes inside the temple. It was essential to keep a low profile. A visit of just a few seconds might be noticed; but on the other hand, if he stayed too long, he ran the risk of his chosen shoes disappearing with their rightful owner before he could swap them.

(4) When entering, decide on the shoes to be swapped as quickly as possible, and when leaving, put them on without hesitation. This had come only with practice. After several imperfect swaps which left him limping, he learned to gauge the size by sight when scoping out the shoes.

(5) Wear only those shoes during the interval between swaps. This was essential in order to maximize the sensation he craved: the lovely way his feet and the "new" shoes gradually melded together. Jiro sometimes walked clear across town for a swap, but it was worth it to feel the eerily refreshing coolness of the strange shoes at the next destination. Now, the only shoes he owned were the most recent swap. This was the price he paid—willingly—for his obsession.

3

The city sighed with relief as the sun disappeared and cool breezes fanned outward in the twilight. Jiro approached his apartment building, climbed several flights of metal exterior stairs and unlocked the flimsy door of his flat. Stepping out of his latest acquisitions in the cramped entryway, he entered the tatami room and opened the tiny fridge to get a plastic bottle of

tea. Then he paused in front of a large black-and-white movie still, of Bogie and Bergman in a clinch in *Casablanca*. Smiling crookedly, he repeated his mantra (in Japanese): "Of all the gin joints, in all the cities, in all the world." *Casablanca* was Jiro's favorite movie, and that line seemed to him to embody the essential absurdity of existence. He always greeted the photograph in this way when he returned to his room.

This little box in the sky, his bolt-hole, was as neat and inconspicuous as Jiro himself. Several black-and-white movie stills tacked on the wall were the only decoration. Beige curtains framing a completely empty balcony, neutral quilt cover and cushions, nondescript brown mat in front of the spick-and-span kitchen alcove—all from the discount store. Black clothing on hangers suspended from the picture rail. A low table with a black laptop, an old-fashioned windup alarm clock, and a few papers. Jiro kept the room clean and cooked for himself, mostly rice and soup. His daily routine was just as rigidly circumscribed—early rising, mornings spent at the computer where he managed websites for a living, afternoons napping or walking around town, evenings watching DVDs of old movies in his room.

Motionless on his futon, the young man blended so well into the room that he was almost invisible.

Jiro's past had been as silent and colorless as his present. His mother and father led unexamined, humdrum lives. It was a mystery how they had mustered up the energy to conceive a child. They called him Jiro, which means "second son," even though he was an only child. He often wondered about this. Any natural baby boisterousness Jiro had shown had been repressed with cold disapproval, until his existence hardly left a dent in their bland self-sufficiency. Neither of them was creative, neither had a temper or a love of animals or a hunger to travel or an appetite for chocolate or any of the other ordinary quirks of humanity. The father went every day to his job under flickering fluorescent lights in a nondescript company in a grimy concrete building in a dreary corner of Osaka. The mother kept the house, did the laundry, and cooked bland, unmemorable meals. Her only discernible character trait was her obsessive neatness, which her son had inherited.

His childhood home had been a silent place, with next to no conversation. He never talked about his school life, just as his father never mentioned the office and his mother never chatted about the dinner menu or neighborhood gossip. He did, however, occasionally hear muffled sobs from the kitchen late at night before his father returned.

As a teenager Jiro went to school, studied, and came home. He made no impression on the other students and received none. Never having seen his parents interact socially with other people, he had no model for doing so. In his final year of high school, after a wartime-era film was shown at the school, Jiro developed an interest in vintage cinema, and even went so far as to join a film club at university. But he never told anyone what he thought about the films, never went out drinking afterwards with fellow club members or participated in the discussions. He got to know the various genres quite well, Japanese, European, and American; he frequented art houses and sent off for DVDs of obscure films—always black-and-white, nothing more recent than 1960.

Shortly after graduating from university, Jiro set himself up as a freelance website designer. He was moderately successful, especially with dull, fact-filled corporate websites. He talked to his clients exclusively by email, a mode of communication that exactly suited his reclusive personality. He had no friends and no visitors; his face-to-face contacts were almost entirely limited to shopkeepers. Jiro was alone, and he liked it that way.

4

"Excuse me!"

The voice behind him was loud and firm. Jiro froze, heart leaping, in the dark entryway of the temple.

"I think those are my shoes," the voice continued.

His face white as paper, Jiro squinted over his shoulder at the well-dressed young guy standing close behind him. His intelligent face was framed in the turned-up collar of a trendy black leather jacket over an expensive white cashmere turtleneck. He looked like a film director. All this registered instantly in Jiro's razor-sharp perception, despite his paralysis. Then his mind supplied one of the two words that would save him. Swallowing convulsively, he croaked, "Mistake."

"Yeah." The guy let a casual, friendly hand fall on Jiro's shoulder, and with the other, he pointed down through the gloom at two almost invisible pairs of black shoes. One pair had Jiro's feet in them.

"Sorry." The other word that would save him fell from Jiro's nerveless lips. He slid his feet out of the shoes and moved aside, struggling to conceal the panic that had flooded him at the young guy's touch. With a smile of acknowledgment, the film-director type slid his feet into his shoes, pushed open the ancient wooden door, and strolled out into the sunshine.

Jiro took a deep, uneven breath and slipped on the other shoes. Their hateful, stale familiarity made him momentarily lightheaded, but he managed to exit the temple with his face set in its usual impassive mask. He walked quickly along, seething with nausea and frustration. Those shoes had been perfect. Why did the guy have to come out at that exact moment? Today's shoe-swap had been a failure, and failure frightened him.

As he walked, Jiro had to admit that his shoe-swapping habit was becoming unmanageable. From his enjoyment of the drama, he had moved on to the mysterious, subtle transition as the strange shoes became his own. Now, increasingly, it was the strangeness itself that gave him the greatest charge of excitement—and the freshness wore off quickly. As the shoes became more familiar, they also became more repulsive, so that lately he was obliged to swap shoes more and more often. He was taking risks, visiting likely temples at more frequent intervals—not even going into the temples themselves, but simply loitering in the entranceway till everyone was out of sight, then rapidly completing the swap and stumbling away without any pretense at nonchalance. It was too risky. He had to get hold of himself.

When he reached his room, he scuffed off the hated shoes convulsively and tore off his socks for good measure, before stepping onto the cool, clean tatami mat with a cry of relief.

5

Early the next morning, after an excruciating sleepless night, Jiro spent a half hour using a kitchen knife to scarify the inside of the hated shoes and make them uncomfortable enough to be wearable. Something inside him watched with incredulous amusement. How had it come to this? The road he had walked the past three years was spiraling down into a place he could scarcely imagine. But he was powerless to stop.

He left his apartment on autopilot and walked aimlessly in the cool dawn. He tried to keep his mind off his feet, but it was no use: his only desire was to find another pair of shoes to swap. He turned corners and crossed streets completely at random, gradually winding upward into the hills east of the city. Suddenly, coming out into a wide square, he found himself at the gate of the immense Kiyomizu Temple complex. This was a place he seldom visited—it was one of the most famous tourist destinations in the city, too crowded for shoe-swapping. But now, in the early light, it was practically deserted. Although the huge wooden gate was shut, a small postern at the side was slightly ajar, and he slipped inside.

Working his way deep into the temple precincts, trudging up stone paths and climbing steps, Jiro began to despair of finding a shoes-off place. Besides, there was no one around—would there be any likely shoes anyway? Not here, not here . . . He turned corner after corner, concentrating so hard that he didn't realize the ground was rising. He shuffled across a wooden deck, came into bright light, and realized he was under the sky. He was standing on the famous balcony. A short distance in front of him was the railing, and beyond was the drop, sheer as a cliff to the fog-wreathed tops of trees far below.

And—could he really be seeing this?—there on the deck, right up against the railing, was a pair of black sports shoes, neatly lined up with their toes pointed toward the drop.

Jiro held his breath as he approached the shoes. Everyone knew the phrase "leaping off Kiyomizu Temple," a proverb which meant coming to a momentous decision. The huge balcony, facing its gulf of air, had been a notorious suicide spot in days gone by.

Everyone also knew that people committing suicide removed their shoes and lined them up carefully before they launched themselves into eternity.

As if in a dream, he walked slowly up to the railing, noticing everything—the tiny droplets of fog clinging to the ancient wood; the pearly sun glowing through gauzy mists; the scent of pines on the hillside. Scarcely breathing, he reached a hand out to the railing. He couldn't bring himself to look over the edge and see what he knew he must—the broken body far below.

Was he really considering swapping shoes with a suicide victim? And what would happen then? Would he be forced to jump as well? But there was no other choice. He could not face the return journey to his flat in the hateful scarified shoes. His heart full of despair, Jiro prepared to swap. He shifted his weight and stepped out of the shoes.

"Hey, man."

A casual, friendly hand fell on his shoulder. The shock made Jiro topple forward, and the hand's grip tightened.

"Look out! This place is dangerous, you know."

Jiro turned in astonishment. It was the film-director type from the day before. The warm, confident voice, the leather jacket, the handsome face, were the same. The intelligent eyes took him in with equal astonishment.

"Hey! Of all the gin joints, in all the cities, in all the world!" the young guy exclaimed. Jiro's whole body jolted at the familiar phrase.

"If it isn't Mr. Mistake-Sorry! What are you doing here?"

Jiro couldn't answer. He gazed down at his stocking feet on the worn, mist-fuzzy boards, at the ruined shoes he had been wearing, and then at the suicide shoes. That brought his tongue back to life.

"A suicide." He pointed down at the shoes, and then over the drop. "Tell someone."

The young guy glanced down and burst out laughing. "What do you mean? These are my shoes. I left them here yesterday. They got a bit dirty during the shoot, so I rinsed them off and left them here to dry. I guess I forgot them when I borrowed another pair from the cameraman. What a laugh! They're probably wetter than ever in all this fog." Jiro's uncomprehending face made him chuckle all over again. "I work here. We're making a film."

Jiro couldn't speak. The stranger looked at him.

"Hey, are you okay? Sorry I startled you. No suicide. I'm right here, I'm fine."

With a huge effort, Jiro formed the word "Casablanca."

"Huh? Oh yeah, that's my favorite movie. I know it by heart. Here's looking at you, kid! Those old black-and-whites are a passion of mine. By the way, my name's Yoshiro."

Something strange was happening to Jiro. "Me too. Casablanca. Me too," he said through the roaring in his ears.

"Want to go get some coffee? You look kind of cold." Yoshiro looked down. "Look at your shoes! They're ruined! You can't wear those. And these ones of mine are still really wet"—stooping to feel the shoes next to the railing.

"That's okay." Jiro determinedly reached down, pulled off his damp socks, and stuck them in his pocket. For the first time in his life, his bare feet touched an exterior surface. The dewdrops prickled his soles. He felt an enormous sigh come straight up from his freed feet. On the way, it melted his frozen chest and loosened his throat. "I don't need shoes."

"Well, all right!" Yoshiro exclaimed. "Let's go." He put an arm around Jiro's shoulders, and they walked off together, Jiro's white bare feet winking in the morning sun.

Author's Note

Each story in this collection is based on some inspiration, for which I am indebted to specific persons or groups. I'd like to explain where these inspirations came from.

The story lines of "A Year of Coffee and Cake" and "Love and Duty" were suggested by anecdotes told to me by members of the Association of Foreign Wives of Japanese.

Those of "Trial by Fire" and "Showa Girl" were suggested by events in the past that have become cherished stories in my husband's family.

"Rhododendron Valley," "Genbei's Curse" and "Three Village Tales" were inspired by actual occurrences in my village in Japan.

"The Mad Kyoto Shoe Swapper" and "Rachel and Leah" are based on personal experiences. "The Turtle Stone" comes from my observation of declining traditional crafts in the city of Kyoto, although this story is not based on any real life sweetshop.

"The Rescuer," "Uncle Trash," and "Watch Again" are modern stories that were suggested by news items set in urban areas.

I'd like to thank my family, friends, and the people that surround me every day, and the richness of my life in Japan in general. Without these experiences, these stories, and the characters in them, would never have come to life.

"Rhododendron Valley" first appeared in *Kyoto Journal* #79.

"The Rescuer" first appeared in edited form in *The Best Asian Short Stories 2018* anthology (Kitaab, Singapore 2018).